Twelve Kisses
Until Christmas

First Published, December, 2016
Printed in the United States of America.

ISBN: 978-0-9963611-4-9

Edited by Danielle Poiesz at Double Vision Editorial
Cover design by Kim Killion of the Killion Group

For more information please see jenniferlohmann.com.

Praise for Jennifer Lohmann

Winning Ruby Heart

"Librarian and author Lohmann . . . has written a remarkable story of a heroine who refuses to let her past mistakes define her future. Lohmann's realistically flawed characters and emotionally compelling plot will resonate with readers who cherish . . . groundbreaking contemporary romances . . ."
—*Booklist*

"Edgy, steamy, and through provoking, this story of two driven, self-centered athletes who have a lot to work through is . . . a compelling and rewarding read."
—*Library Journal*
A Top Pick, Seal of Excellence Award Winner and 2014 Reviewers' Choice Award Winner from *RT Book Reviews*

The First Move

"My only wish is that the book had gone on longer. This was a great, unexpected read, and it's on my short list for best category romance of 2013."
—An All About Romance Desert Island Keeper

"There are so many intricate pieces to this story, all of them sharp and some of them painful, but well worth reading."
– Smart Bitches Trashy Books

"There are moments of brilliance and heartbreak that just damn near ripped my heart out."

—The Misadventures of Super Librarian

Reservations for Two

"Lively dialogue, relatable characters and exquisite descriptions of Polish sausage and pierogies make this a scrumptious tale."

—*RT Book Reviews*

2013 Best First Book in the National Readers' Choice Awards

A Promise for the Baby

"This introspective, character-driven story is rich with family and American Polish culture."

—*Library Journal*

Weekends in Carolina

"*Weekends in Carolina* includes complex characters and an inside look at small farming that many readers will find fascinating."

—*RT Book Reviews*

Dedication

To the Ginger Viking. I quite literally could not have done this summer without you. You make it all possible.

Twelve Kisses Until Christmas

BY

JENNIFER LOHMANN

Chapter One

OUT OF THE small gap between the dirty, cheap, cream-colored curtains, Selina Lumina watched her stepfather park in the driveway, leaving both left wheels on the snow covering their front lawn. She let the curtains fall closed and contemplated her possible exits. The Christmas lights her mom had strung on the front stoop the Friday after Thanksgiving would make it easy to watch Gary stagger up the front walk before he stumbled on the ice on the stairs, but there was no way he was drunk enough she could slip past him unnoticed.

Her heart beat a little faster, fear making it difficult to swallow, slowing her movements, and clouding her ability to come up with a plan. Two facts lingered at the front of her mind, shoving out everything else, even as she tried to take deep breaths and *think*: Gary was drunk. And her mom was at work.

The hard fall of Gary's boots on the front step broke through the panic that had frozen her in place, and she bolted for her room. She shoved every piece of furniture she passed into the path between the front door and her room, tripping over her own feet as she hurried. She banged her shin against the coffee table and took the corner so quickly that she smashed her hand into the edge of the wall.

"Ouch." She cradled her hand to her chest, swallowing her holler. Tears welled in her eyes at the pain in her wrist bone, but she didn't slow down. Terror burned through her body, propelling her forward. She burst into her bedroom just as she heard Gary slide his key into the lock at the front door. Both doors slammed shut at the same time. Selina twisted the small lock in her doorknob while Gary ran into the stool by the front door.

His first obstacle.

The stool had stopped him once before. A kitchen chair had stopped him another time. And the ironing board yet another. As she sank against her bedroom door, her back against the hard wood, she knew that no piece of furniture she put in Gary's way would stop him forever.

Her cheeks were wet as she dropped her head between her knees. Gary had always been a creep, but he'd gotten worse since losing his job. To make up for the lost income, her mom had started working more, and he'd come to Selina for company. A couple of strange touches, some innuendos that had made her cringe, and then he'd grabbed her arm and pulled her toward him.

Yelling and kicking had worked that time. Gary had been apologetic the next morning before going out to the library to apply for jobs. He'd even gotten one and worked at it for a month, going out and drinking with his buddies while her mom worked nights, and then he'd gotten fired again. The drinking started earlier and earlier in the day, and her mom worked later and later. Innuendos had changed to outright statements about needing to "get some" and her mom not being around.

She covered her mouth with her hand to cover her breathing. Her car was parked out front, but maybe if he couldn't hear her, he would think that she had gone out with friends. She used to go out with her friends, especially before she'd adopted her mom's solution and started waitressing as many hours as Babe would let her. If she wasn't at school, she was working.

Gary ran into another piece of furniture, and she cringed. Tonight had been one of those nights when her exhaustion had caught up with her and she'd needed to come home to sleep.

He pounded on the door. "Selina!" he slurred. "I know you're in there. Let me in, baby."

Baby. Bile rose up in her throat at the endearment. Gary always started off nice. Baby. Sweetie. Good time.

Gag.

Before the night was over, *baby* would turn to *bitch* and he'd stop promising her that she'd like it. They both knew he didn't care if she would like it.

God, her eyes hurt. The rims, her eyelids, and the skin under her eyes all ached. She hadn't known it was possible to be this exhausted. But even if Gary stopped twisting the handle of her bedroom door right now, she wouldn't sleep again tonight.

The door rattled as he banged on it, the fading bruises on her back still tender from the last time he'd gotten this drunk and she'd been home. The tiny door lock wouldn't hold him for long. Sometime in the future, he'd be in the perfect spot between drunk enough to try something and sober enough to be able to kick the door down.

She glanced across the room, in case tonight was the night. There, sitting under the window, was her backpack with a spare toothbrush, pajamas, jeans, her favorite sweatshirt, and twenty dollars. It wasn't much, but it would be enough to hold her over until she could get back home and pack up the rest of her stuff.

Gary's footsteps retreated down the hall, and she eased her way back to a stand. She'd fallen for the retreating-footsteps trick once. This time, she picked up her nightstand and moved it in front of her door.

The backpack and escape was a nice idea, but the truth was that she had nowhere to go, making fortification more realistic than retreat.

After she pushed everything she could think of in front of her door, she lifted her heavy limbs into bed and curled up in a tight ball, her eyes zeroed in on the door while she waited for her stepfather to pass out.

Like she did every other night she'd been trapped in her room, trapped in her house, and trapped in her life, she imagined the moment when all her hard work paid off and she was handed her diploma. That diploma, and the nursing job that would come with it, was her out.

Out of this house. Out of this town. Out of this life.

Whatever banged on the door next couldn't have been Gary's hand. Or his foot. The bang, and the accompanying crack in the wood, indicated something much bigger. Panic coursed through her, and very real and very scary possibilities drove her out of her bed. As the doorframe cracked behind her, Selina grabbed her coat and her backpack. She didn't bother to hide her groans as she shoved at the window. She welcomed the cold air that blasted her face.

Her bedroom door broke open and crashed to the ground just as Selina was slipping through the open window and out into the night. The freezing early-December air made goose pimples rise on her bare arms, her breath visible. She raced around the side of the house to her car and climbed in. Besides the clothes in her backpack, she had a blanket in the car. She could sleep in the diner's parking lot if she had to, but she was never going back to that house.

Chapter Two

"CURTIS, YOU'RE NOT listening to me," Marc Murcowski said into the overly warm air of the car as he navigated the twisting road up and around the mountain.

"What's the big problem with Terry?" Curtis asked.

Terry had been their pet name for the encrypted text message app they'd sold for millions of dollars. Who knows what it was called now? Something that sounded more secretive, no doubt, and probably boring, too.

"Right now, Terry needs mutual contact-list entries to generate a key. But I've figured out a way around our problem." He tapped his steering wheel excitedly. The solution was so simple, so elegant; they should have seen it months ago. Maybe they could have sold the company for more if they had.

The silence on the other end of the line lasted long enough that Marc glanced at the screen on his dash to make sure he still had service. Just as he was about to reach over and shake his phone—not that it would have any effect, but doing *something* would make him feel better and he couldn't shake his best friend and former business partner into listening to him—Curtis cleared his throat.

"It's not *our* problem," he said. "The contact-list entry is *my problem.* You. Sold. Terry."

The way Curtis enunciated every word made the joints of Marc's jaw ache, but he didn't give in to his irritation. Curtis had something Marc wanted. Namely, Curtis still had access to the app they'd developed and Marc didn't.

"Technically," he said, struggling to keep his voice jolly, "we both sold the company. You simply chose to stay on after all the checks were written."

Marc slowed his SUV as he approached the next hairpin turn. He should be appreciating the scenery of the Idaho mountains in the early winter. After all, he had cancelled the lease on his Seattle apartment and driven off with the intent of seeing the country and skiing at all the best resorts. But pine trees and snowy mountaintops were competition for the way his mind had rolled over the contact-list problem since he'd driven out of town in search of . . .

Maybe that was the issue. He didn't know what he was looking for other than something else to occupy his mind. Some intricate, interesting problem to solve. Something with a minor detail out of place where the solution would hit him over the head and a small edit in the code would make an audience of investors open their checkbooks.

A life of leisure had turned out to be really fucking

boring. And it had only been a week.

"And you were given the chance to stay on when we sold Terry, too. You refused."

Marc took the next turn as Curtis was silent again. They'd been friends long enough for Marc to imagine what his friend was doing. Curtis was probably sitting at his desk—before they'd sold Terry, they'd both been at their desk 95 percent of their waking hours—rolling his eyes at the wall. Curtis always rolled his eyes when he thought he was right but the other person was still arguing.

"Satellite lost," the GPS woman said in her tinny voice. For the past two hours, it was all she'd been able to say. Occasionally she'd say, "Satellite found," but mostly lost.

"Come on, Betty." He'd started calling her that yesterday, the second time he'd made a hairpin turn in the middle of nowhere in Idaho, centermost middle of nowhere state. He and Curtis had this joke that if you named technology, it would behave better. 'Cause it felt loved, 'cause you were furthering its ability to take over the world *Matrix*-style, 'cause it made swearing at it more satisfying. The two of them had had different ideas about *why* you had to name technology.

Marc named technology because he loved it. Curtis wanted to take over the world. They both liked swearing.

"Look," he said to the screen as he pulled his brand-new Land Rover over to the side of the road. "I'm sorry it took me a day to give you a name. I get it. You're still mad. But I've named you. I've apologized. Now just tell me where the fuck I'm supposed to go."

That request wasn't a complete joke. When he'd started out this morning, he hadn't put a destination into the GPS. His grand plan for the past week had been to drive around, pull over at every overlook and random historical site, and reconcile his whirring mind to his new situation as he drove from ski resort to ski resort. So far, all he'd done was solve Terry's biggest hitch and call Curtis.

Once safely as far over to the side of the road as he dared, he reached for one of the phones sitting in the passenger seat. Veronica, his Verizon Samsung had no bars. He tossed it back, grabbing for Megan, his AT&T Motorola phone. He huffed. No bars. His favorite phone was failing him now, too. He set it on the seat next to the Samsung and snatched up the last phone, Holly, his Sprint HTC. She didn't have bars, either. When he pitched Holly back to the seat, she bounced once, then slid off onto the floor.

By now, Curtis had to have realized that the call had been dropped. Marc sighed. Well, at least his friend would have extra time to consider that Marc had a solution to their problem and would come to his senses. Because Marc needed something to do in empty hotel rooms after driving around all day.

"I owe you another apology, Betty," he said to the GPS. Having lost his call with Curtis, he only had the machines to talk to. "It's not your fault we're lost.

Clearly an asteroid has hit Earth somewhere, wiping out all possible technology, leaving me to fend for myself in the wilderness."

An opportunity, the fucking voice in the back of his head said. *Drive out of here, head south, and announce to Curtis and everyone on that huge company campus that you can write the code to save the planet.*

He laid his head in his hands on the steering wheel and looked to the passenger seat. His three phones represented all the communication he had with the outside world anymore, short of the brief conversations with hotel desk clerks and fast-food cashiers. Which, he reminded himself, was what he had wanted. After the tight living of writing Terry and the stress of selling her, he had *needed* time to himself, to figure out who he was and what he wanted to do next. Disappearing into the woods was a time-honored path to discovery. It wasn't as though he'd be bored forever. He had ski vacations booked through the rest of the winter. The restlessness would pass.

He shifted into reverse and turned the car around. He'd head down the mountain. There were towns at the base where he could take a break from driving. And when he landed back in civilization and checked his e-mail, he told himself, there would be something from Curtis saying he wanted Marc's help.

Marc drove until Betty announced the glories of satellite reception. Then, before he could lose his connection to the modern world, he asked his favorite phone to give him directions to food. As backup, he asked Betty, too.

They directed him to the parking lot of an old-fashioned, run-down diner. His SUV crunched and bumped in the pothole-studded asphalt. The fissures in the earth must have been left over from previous winters, since it was only the beginning of December and winter hadn't attacked northern Idaho with the full force of her power yet. His eyes skimmed the building as he made his way toward it. The *E* in the neon OPEN sign was out, and the *N* flickered. The door opened just fine, though, and it smelled like bacon and sausage inside, so he sat himself, as the sign instructed.

A waitress in her late twenties walked up to him with a menu in one hand and a globe of coffee in the other. Her bright, yellow-blond hair was bluntly cut at her chin and swung about her face as she walked. Her red lips were turned down, and when she got closer, he realized that she was younger than he'd first thought, early twenties probably.

She looked tired as she set the menu in front of him and reached out to turn up his coffee cup. She had dark, puffy circles under her eyes, and her face looked wan. Even her shoulders sagged. The woman seemed exhausted, the kind of tired that sank into one's bones and made each step feel like a slog through mud.

"Welcome to Babe's," she said, pouring coffee before asking if he wanted decaf, or even coffee at all. Marc was tempted to invite her to sit down—before she *fell* down—but wasn't smooth enough to pull that off without sounding like a creep or making her feel uncomfortable. He decided to make an extra effort to be a good customer instead.

And leave a good tip.

"We're out of the steak for steak and eggs. The orange juice is fresh squeezed." That bit was said with an edge to her voice, as if she would be the one squeezing it and he would be the one regretting ordering it. Not only did she seem weary from lack of sleep, but she seemed weary from life, he judged from the way light seemed to try—and failed—to flicker in her eyes. "Everything else is on the menu. I'll give you a minute to look it over. Ya want water?"

If she was as worn-down as he was guessing, it was no wonder she sounded eager to get rid of him. Perversely, he liked the careless tone she addressed him with. Excellent customer service was nice, but the barely-on-the-edge of polite waitress with cherry-red lips was far more interesting. Especially one who was as cute as she was in her short skirt and ruffled white apron.

"No water," he said.

She wobbled slightly as she turned to walk away, her skirt swinging almost as much as her hair. God, it barely covered her butt. He looked up, embarrassed to be staring at the backs of her thighs.

"Wait," he called to her back. "What should I get?"

When she turned around to look at him, her face had softened and there was the hint of a smile on her lips, giving him a glimpse of the woman she might be underneath her fatigue. When he and Curtis had been spending days and nights building their app, he'd had times when no amount of coffee would help to keep his eyelids open. And here she was, even managing a smile. It was impressive. And intriguing.

"Get the Elk Chips. Roasted potatoes, scrambled eggs, peppers, sausage, and cheese all in one big pile, topped with sour cream and salsa. It's basically everything you could want in a breakfast."

"And what if I'm a sweet guy?" he asked, attempting an easy, flirtatious tone, something he'd never had much success with. However, now that he'd seen her smile, he didn't want her to leave the table and he was going to give it everything he had.

She mustered another small smile. "Huckleberry pancakes. Babe picks the berries herself—at patches she won't tell anyone else about. If you've never had real huckleberries, you should get those. Babe makes the huckleberry syrup, too."

"I'll have that, then. I want you to remember my sweetness." God, he'd meant that sincerely, but even he could hear that he sounded like an ass covered in slime.

Her smile disappeared, replaced by raised eyebrows and suspiciously narrowed eyes. "Was that supposed to be a pickup line?"

He shrugged, chagrined. "I'm just trying to make your day better, not worse."

Her eyebrows remained up. "So pickup line or not?"

JENNIFER LOHMANN

Smooth, he wasn't. She probably heard cracks like that all the time from random men who walked into Babe's Diner and wanted to see a smile on her face.

"Somewhere in between," he offered, trying to verbally back away without fully retreating.

She continued to look unimpressed. "You know, pickup lines are almost never successful with women, and especially not when delivered halfheartedly."

He laughed at the truth of the matter. The town sign had said the population was 692. On his way to the diner he'd seen a vet's office, a bar, a hardware store, and a steakhouse, but no McDonald's. So it wasn't that she was sick of all the strangers coming in and hitting on her, he realized. It was that he'd tried, struck out, and then was being a coward about it.

"You're right," he said, shaking his head at himself. "Well, here's the honest truth. I suck at being smooth. If I'd wanted to impress you, I should have talked nerdy to you. I'm good at that."

To his surprise—and apparently to hers, too—she laughed. Her entire face brightened. For a brief moment, the dark circles were gone from under her eyes and the little Christmas bells hanging from her ears jingled. Pleasure filled his chest. He was as proud as if he'd just dragged an enormous dead animal to the cave of the woman he was trying to impress. At least he knew enough not to bang on his chest.

"That was better," she said with a smile and a shake of her holly-tipped pen. "Huckleberry pancakes it is.

Comes with bacon or sausage."

"Bacon, please."

She nodded, a hint of a smile still present on her lips. "It'll go with your sweetness."

This time, when she walked away, he didn't feel guilty for enjoying the view before picking up his mug of coffee. He took a sip, prepared to grimace at the stale, pre-ground coffee, and was stunned by the rich, smooth liquid that jolted him awake. He pulled Megan out of his pocket and skimmed through his e-mail. A couple of messages from his dating app profile, which he deleted without looking at. Some e-mails thanking him for entering some contest—his mother's doing. And there, buried in the midst of the junk, was the e-mail he had been expecting from Curtis.

He sat back in his seat and read the message. Curtis thanked him for the offer of work, then told him that they would be sure to contact him if they had lingering issues with Terry that Curtis couldn't solve. *But right now, we're good,* he'd written.

He hit the "reply" button. *We're a team,* he typed, then deleted it. They had been a team. Curtis would be sure to point out *again* that they had both been asked to stay with Terry in her new home and Marc had turned the offer down.

Better to stay with the simple, *We should talk again.* Curtis had always thought they were good. Throughout the entire building process, it had been Marc who had pushed for tighter code, better security, more encryption, fewer holes. Curtis's strength was writing code; Marc's was fixing it.

Good editors were never given the credit they were due. Or that had been how Marc had felt when they were in negotiations and all the attention had been given to Curtis.

"Here ya go."

The waitress's voice startled him out of the lies he was about to start telling himself. He had been offered a job, just as Curtis had, and he'd rejected it because he hadn't felt like his ego was being stroked enough. That impulsive rejection was his fault. It's why he was on the outside, an elegant solution running circles in his mind, and Curtis was on the inside, ignoring him.

"Hey, this smells good." The bacon was thick and crispy, not too much fat. The purple syrup smelled sweet and tart, like it would make him pucker and his dentist cringe in the best possible way. The pancakes themselves smelled like butter.

"Babe knows what she's doing," his waitress answered as she took a step back, putting distance between them, their shared laughter nothing but a memory.

"Can I ask you a question?"

She raised a pale eyebrow at him, and he held his hands up. "I'm not trying to hit on you, I promise."

Doubt shadowed her face. Maybe it was due to how tired she was, but reactions flittered across her face like a movie he would never get bored watching.

"Okay," he said, waving a hand. "Men who aren't

hitting on women always swear they aren't. It's the oldest trick in the book. But look, I'm at loose ends until Saturday and am driving around exploring stuff. Got any local recommendations?"

"What kind of stuff?" Her face relaxed a little. Though she still looked tired, he could tell that curiosity had caught hold of her.

"Anything, really. I'm between jobs for a while and packed my winter with sightseeing and skiing. I came to Idaho to see some cool things, so maybe you know of some cool things." God, he sounded like an idiot. Several million dollars in the bank and technology articles about his work hadn't done anything for his ability to talk to women. Confidence in one didn't mean confidence in the other.

"You came *here* to see cool things? In the winter?" Her head jutted forward, and her brow furrowed. He'd had a full-sized poodle as a kid and she'd had the same look whenever he'd asked her to do something ridiculous. He hid his smile at the thought. His waitress probably wouldn't appreciate the comparison, even though he'd loved that dog.

"Technically, it's still fall," he corrected. "For another week or so."

The sanctimony he could hear in his own voice opened her mouth completely, either in confusion or disbelief, he couldn't tell. But the only sound that came out was a huff. He'd knocked the words right out of her.

Smooth, as always. Correcting strangers was his most

charming move. Worked . . . never. It had never worked.

"Sorry," he said, trying for as much sincerity as he'd had smug correctness. "I can be a pompous ass. I'd say ignore me, but *I* wouldn't be able to ignore me, especially when I'm at my worst." He paused and then changed the subject. "But yeah . . . It's cold, but I couldn't help the timing, and I've never been to Idaho. There's got to be something around here I can check out. The biggest ball of yarn. A Jolly Green Giant statue. Something."

Finally, she shook her head. "Well, if you are hitting on me, you're doing a terrible job of it." She sounded amazed, so there was that. He'd leave an impression, and sometimes that was all he could hope for.

He laughed at himself and his own failures. "What's even more sad is that this would be one of my better efforts. If I were hitting on you right now, that is. Which I'm not."

She laughed with him, their connection from earlier reestablished. Then she turned her long neck to yell over her shoulder. "Hey, Babe, is the submarine museum open?"

"Now? No," came an incredulous voice from the kitchen. Babe, he gathered, was the diner's namesake and the woman responsible for the amazing smells.

"Submarine museum? That sounds cool." He hadn't expected anything so interesting when he'd made his plans.

When she shook her head, he caught sight of little

red bows at the top of her bell earrings. "It's a museum in an old Navy jail. They did training up here back in World War II. And they test submarines there, if you can believe it. But the museum is closed in the winter."

"What about the Wolf People?" Babe called out from the kitchen.

"Wolf People?" He liked technology, but he'd been staring at computers for too many years. Animals would be a nice break. "Now *that* sounds interesting."

"I guess. We went there every year on field trips, same as the submarine museum, so it seems like an old hat to me." She nodded her head toward his plate. "You should eat your food. It's going to get cold."

Obediently, he cut some pancake away from the rest with the side of his fork. "Tell me about the Wolf People. I'll eat. You talk."

She shrugged, looking both less irritated and less tired than she had when he'd first sat down. Maybe not chipper, but her face was no longer drawn and she'd lost the wobble he'd seen in her when she'd gone back to turn in his order. "The Wolf People is an organization north of here. There are some twenty wolves in a closed park. You can take a tour, and there's a gift shop."

Marc nodded and swallowed his food. "These are delicious. Good pick."

His waitress inclined her head to the kitchen. "It's Babe. She's such a good cook." The rest of the sentence went unsaid, but he heard it. Babe's talents were wasted on this tiny town in the middle of nowhere and—maybe he heard this in the waitress's tone, too—so were the talents and interests of his waitress.

He wondered what her talents are. Was she happy in this small town? Did she want to leave? He'd desperately wanted to leave his own small town, but not everyone he'd gone to school with had felt the same way.

Whatever he was hearing in his waitress's tone of voice, though, he let it alone. Athol, Idaho was a blip in the course of his trip. He was passing through her life as much as he was passing through this town while he decided what to do next. And spent some of his sudden wealth on skiing the best snow on earth. He was searching for something, but that didn't mean he wasn't going to enjoy himself.

"All right. You've sold me on the Wolf People. And I'll drive by the museum. Even if it's not open, maybe there's something I can see. They don't test submarines in the air, do they? 'Cause seeing a zeppelin would be awesome."

"No," she said, laughing. "Lake Pend Orielle is there. And it's a state park. The whole place is pretty. It's cold, but you'll probably see people horseback riding and, since it's clear, flying model airplanes. Maybe a model zeppelin," she said, and he could swear her voice was flirtatious.

He cut aside more of his delicious pancake—a bigger piece this time—and scooped up more of the syrup. "That sounds worth the drive. Pretty is good."

She blushed, like maybe he was referring to her, even

though he hadn't intended to. Or maybe she was just tired and here he was, reading more into her face and posture than was really there. He was a stranger and she was a waitress, used to dealing with people, even if being on this out-of-the-way mountain meant those people weren't usually strangers.

But she *was* pretty, and he wanted to talk to her for as long as she was willing to stand here and talk to him. "Okay. Naval museum, state park, and wolves. Anything else?"

She cocked her head. "You're going to be driving all over Hell's Half Acre just to see those three things. Are you sure you want more suggestions?"

"I've got all day and no place I need to be until Saturday." He picked up a piece of bacon and looked at it. It was thick and studded with pepper. Between the waitress and the diner, he would consider passing through Athol again.

"How about this?" he said, thinking both of the delicious breakfast and of his pretty waitress. "How about I see those things, then come back for dinner and tell you what I thought of them. Then you'll know if you should suggest them to the next passing stranger."

"We don't get many passing strangers," she said, her eyes twinkling with humor, the tiredness he'd seen earlier mostly gone.

"Of course not. All the more reason to be prepared for the next one that comes in. You can practice on me. I volunteer. In fact, I insist," he said, pounding a fist on the table as if it were a gavel.

She waved him off, obviously trying not to give in to a smile. "I'm only supposed to work the morning shift."

"As I said, the food's good, so I'll come back for dinner anyway and hope that you're still here to listen to my adventures."

"If I'm not here, Jesse eats dinner here almost every night. He always needs some company."

So do I. The thought entered Marc's head so quickly he almost didn't notice its entry and attempt to set up camp. He shook his head to dislodge the drivel.

"Don't want to tell your tales to Jesse?" she asked.

"Jesse sounds all right," he said, turning one palm up on the table, which was cool under the back of his hand. "I'd rather tell my tales to you, but I told you that I wasn't trying to pick you up and I'm trying to stick to my word."

His honesty was rewarded with a blinding, full-wattage smile from his waitress, the first one he'd seen all morning. No tiredness lingered in her eyes, and her shoulders weren't slumped anymore.

"Thank you," she said. "I like a man who sticks to his word."

Now Marc was regretting saying anything. Of course, when he'd been trying to flirt with her and get her to smile, she'd gotten irritated and defensive. Now that he was just trying to be himself and talk with her, he was being rewarded. He wasn't so blind as to not notice the lesson here.

Not that he'd get a chance to make use of said lesson. He was enjoying his waitress's smiles particularly because he didn't get the feeling that she had much of an opportunity to show them. He liked the way he felt as though he could let his guard down around her, not to mention that her mix of suspicion and friendliness made him want to know more about her.

He wouldn't get to, of course. She'd told him that he didn't even have a chance at another conversation, much less insight into her history and personality.

Just as well. His father had always said that the best way to figure out what to do with your life was to disappear into the wilderness and let nature tell you. His father hadn't said anything about taking someone else along for the ride.

"Anyway," she said, patting the Formica table and nearly brushing his own hand, which was still resting there, palm up. "I'll leave you alone so that you can eat. Pay at the front and holler if you need more coffee."

A couple walked into the diner as soon as his waitress walked away, but the place had never felt emptier.

Chapter Three

"HEY." A STRONG, reassuring hand pressed into Selina's shoulder. "Want a cup of coffee?"

Selina looked up into the warm eyes of her boss, Babe. "I do, but I shouldn't have one. I need to try to sleep tonight."

The woman rubbed Selina's shoulder and down her arm. "Do you need a *place* to sleep tonight?"

Babe could look intimidating in the kitchen, especially when standing there with a knife, her white apron covering a generous bosom and an almost as generous stomach. But the people close to her knew that her heart took up as much space as her body. Her husband was known to say that her body wasn't big enough for all the things he loved about his wife.

"Yes, but I don't want to be anywhere my mom will think to look. She'll ask me to come home, and I can't." She couldn't face her mom and the hurt she'd surely caused when she'd run off. But she couldn't face Gary or that house again, either.

The worst part would be the show her mom would make of it. She would put her hand against her forehead, moan about her ungrateful daughter and all the work she and Gary had put into raising her. Selina didn't have a clue why her mom even wanted her around. As far as she could tell, the very fact that she was living in the same town where she grew up, in the same house even, was a disappointment to everything her mother had worked for.

Drama—her mother's specialty.

At first, Selina had been happy when her mom had started working more hours. There'd been less yelling. Of course, now she'd take the yelling if it meant that she wasn't home alone with Gary.

"There's that spare bedroom at my sister's." Babe's sister lived an hour north, almost spitting distance from the Canadian border.

"I'm a little afraid to drive up there, as tired as I am." It was clear now, but a storm was supposed to be rolling in tonight. Driving on the highway in blinding snow was treacherous enough when wide-awake.

"Plus, better that you don't know where I am when my family comes knocking." For all her mom and Gary's fake concern, Selina brought home an income they both needed. Gary was an angry, abusive drunk, but he wasn't an idiot. And he certainly wasn't lazy when it came to making sure someone was around to buy groceries.

"Why haven't you moved? Out of the house, at least?" Babe kept her hand on Selina's back so she knew her boss wasn't being judgmental or critical, just merely asking the same questions Selina asked herself almost every night.

For all her big talk about never going back to that house again, she knew she probably would. A couple of nights sleeping in her car, a couple of nights feeling guilty when Gary knocked on her friends' houses at two in the morning, and a couple of calls from her mom saying the electric bill was late. That would be all it would take, though she'd buy a bar to put across her door.

"Money. Isn't that the reason anyone ever does anything?" As far as she could tell, money was the reason Gary didn't just move out, not when Selina and her mom paid the mortgage, the bills, and for most of the groceries.

All those bills ate into Selina's escape money, too, plus there was tuition for her community college classes, the expense of driving to Sandpoint, the nearest town with a community college, textbooks, a laptop . . . Funds drained out of her bank account almost as quickly as she was able to put them in, especially since not everyone left as nice a tip as the man from this morning had. That money would fill up her gas tank, at least.

"Sorry I can't pay you more."

"Thanks, Babe, but I get it."

Babe's Diner, like all the other businesses in this town, made almost no money. No one in town made much money. There was a naval testing center and . . . well, nothing else for people to do for work. Everyone's fingernails were worn to the quick in an effort to make ends meet. No one had anything extra.

"I'll get out of here," she said, trying to sound hopeful.

Someday.

She was taking a survey of art history class, and while she'd probably end up being a nurse—practicality trumped dreams—she liked to imagine what it would be like to work in an art gallery. She'd looked up pictures of galleries online, all white walls and brightly colored art. She'd have a signature pair of black boots and . . .

She sighed. Who was she kidding? Nursing was a good, important, practical job. She'd probably even find it satisfying. Even if dreams were more fun.

Babe rubbed her back. "I'll get you that cup of coffee anyway. You look tired enough that you'll sleep even if I hooked you up to a caffeine IV."

"Thanks, Babe."

Selina didn't drink the coffee Babe set in front of her, though. Instead, she wrapped her hands around the mug and let the warmth relax the muscles in her arms as she watched the black liquid ripple when a tear rolled off her cheek. She was tired—that's all the tears were.

And frustrated. And worn-out. And sad.

But those tears weren't hopeless tears. As long as she was passing her community college courses, she still had a chance to get out eventually. Climbing a mountain happened one step at a time. Transfer credits happened one *class* at a time.

The bell above the diner door tinkled. Out of habit,

Selina looked at it, even though her shift was over. The man who'd left her that twenty-dollar tip was walking through the door. He caught her gaze, and he blinked several times before giving her a tentative smile and walking over.

"You said you wouldn't be here," he said, standing above her table in a reversal of their roles from this morning.

"Jesse hasn't shown up yet. I didn't want you to think no one in town was interested in your adventures." She managed a small smile. Having a stranger see tears streaking down her cheeks was embarrassing. She could at least hope the smile would distract him.

Whether or not it did, he had the decency to at least pretend he didn't notice that she'd been crying, answering her smile with a floppy one of his own.

Floppy was a good adjective for the stranger. His wavy, dark-brown hair flopped over his forehead, his neck, and his ears. His nose was a little too big and the tip of it too round for his face, but it—and his thick eyebrows—gave his face character and intelligence. It was that intelligence she'd reacted to earlier, flirting back instead of slinking off to the mop closet for a nap. And it was that intelligence that answered the question that had been lurking in the back of her mind since he'd walked in that morning.

Yup. He was cute.

"Can I sit down?" he asked, gesturing at the empty seat across from her.

"Yeah," she said, nodding. She needed company—someone cute, smart, and not creepy. Someone from outside this little forgotten town.

"You still working?"

"What?" She looked down, a little surprised to see that she was still wearing the Creamsicle-colored outfit. "No. I just don't want to go home." That was less embarrassing to admit that than to tell him she didn't really have a home anymore.

"Can I buy you dinner? No strings. Just dinner." His eyes gleamed with sincerity.

"I work here. Babe'll feed me for free."

"I'll take you somewhere else, then. I saw a steakhouse."

"No, not there." Gary liked to go there, and the owner liked her stepfather's nasty, mean sense of humor. "There's China Garden."

"Is it good?"

She shrugged. "It's good compared to the other Chinese restaurants in the area. They have pork and seeds."

"Pork and seeds?"

"Pieces of smoked pork you dip in hot mustard, then sesame seeds."

His eyes widened, and for a moment she wondered if he would make fun of the small town and its Chinese restaurant where pork and seeds were the highlight. But he only said, "All right," and started sliding out of his chair.

"Do you need directions?" she asked as she pushed

herself out of the booth.

"Nah. I've got a GPS and three phones. If I get lost, I deserve to starve." Then he laughed.

"What's so funny?"

"I was lost this morning with those three phones and GPS. I had no idea where I was. But I found Babe's, so it worked out in the end."

"Oh." The subtle compliment made her heart feel big and the tearstains on her cheeks unimportant. "I just need to change. I'll meet you there in a couple minutes."

He hesitated for a moment, and she wondered if he was worried she'd stand him up. "What's your name?" he asked instead.

"Selina."

"I'm Marc. See you at the China Garden in ten minutes, Selina."

She nodded. It was just dinner and he was a stranger who was going to leave town at any moment, but the night was looking up.

SHE PUSHED OPEN the large wooden door and scanned the restaurant for a now-familiar head of hair and the tops of slightly-too-big ears. The restaurant looked the same as it had since she was a child—the same red vinyl booths, the same red carpet with gold flecks, the same red Chinese lanterns with black script hanging from the ceiling. As a nod to the season, "Silent Night" was playing and there was fake greenery above the cash register.

She almost missed Marc, whose head was blocked by the salad bar in the middle of the restaurant.

"Hey," she said as she slid into the booth. Even though this wasn't a date, her heart fluttered.

Of course, if it wasn't a date, what the hell was it?

"Hey," he said back. "You look nice, but I miss the Popsicle look."

"Thanks." She was wearing the same clothes she'd had on last night, when she'd been driving around town, but the jeans fit well and she liked the funny cartoon potato on her purple T-shirt. It was silly, but she needed a little silly in her life.

"Don't get me wrong, the uniform was cute, too."

"Hey," she said, pursing her lips against her smile at his compliment. "I thought this was a no-strings-attached dinner." Marc's awkwardness and the way he laughed at himself about it had been part of what had put her at ease originally. But Gary never took no for an answer, and she needed to make sure Marc did, even if it was just dinner.

"What?" His eyes crossed in confusion for a brief second before realization dawned. "Oh, the compliments. Men in this town must operate under different rules from what I was taught if compliments mean more than what they are at face value. You're pretty. I like your company. I invited you to dinner for the latter, but the former doesn't hurt. But all I want is someone to talk to.

I've been driving alone for a while."

"Okay." She shook her head, more at herself than at him. "It's been a rough night and a long day. I'm not normally so suspicious."

"None of us are at our best when we're tired, and you seemed exhausted even this morning. If it makes you more comfortable and more willing to keep me company, be as suspicious as you like. I'll be over here, keeping my hands to myself." He was smiling, and the light in his eyes was both sympathetic and friendly.

Maybe she really could trust him. Maybe he was exactly who he claimed to be and would be and do what he said he would.

There weren't many people in her life she could say that about.

The waitress came to take their order then. Selina ordered pork egg foo young—her favorite—and Marc ordered chow mein and pork and seeds.

"I'm curious about those pork and seeds," he said after the waitress left.

"I'm guessing it's not authentic if you've never had any."

He waved her off. "Or maybe it's incredibly authentic, which is why you can only get it at this restaurant."

She laughed, pleased with the way he turned her inexperience back to compliment her. "Not just here. It's an Idaho Chinese-food specialty. You can get pork and seeds at Costco."

"Nothing more authentic than that." His gentle

teasing put a smile in his tone, even though he'd said the words with a straight face.

"You can comment on their authenticity after you eat them."

She was smiling so much her cheeks hurt. Marc was better than a distraction. Even though she still didn't know where she was sleeping tonight, she was actually enjoying herself, which she wouldn't have thought possible an hour ago.

"Fair," he said, inclining his head.

The waitress came back almost immediately with the appetizer. Marc stared for a moment before laughing. He had a nice, cheerful laugh. Even with his uncertainty about the pork and seeds, there was no indication that he was laughing *at* her or at Idaho's regional variations on Chinese food. Instead, like her, he was facing change in his life and the joy of a simple pleasure was a welcome relief.

It had been a long time since Selina could say she'd felt *joy* in life, and Marc's was contagious.

"It's literally pork and seeds," he said, a smile beaming across his face.

"That's what I said," she pointed out on a laugh, picking up a thin slice of pork, its exterior pink—from being smoked, she always assumed, but food coloring was just as likely. "Watch me. You dip it in the mustard, then in the seeds, and it's delicious. Authenticity be damned."

Marc followed her lead and tried a bite. "This is

good. And here I was thinking dinner with you couldn't get any better."

She raised a brow at him. "Do you have a stock set of lines you use on women?"

"Only the pretty ones," he said with a wink that magically made him seem both goofier and cuter at the same time.

Maybe it was because she was tired. Or maybe it was the pleasure streaming through her veins that she hadn't felt in what seemed like years. Or maybe it was the way he pursed his lips when he'd spoken, as though he hadn't thought he was going to get away with it. Whatever it was, she couldn't help laughing.

He grinned. "They don't usually work so well. Actually, they usually fail and I end up stumbling over my tongue like an ass. But if you keep smiling, I'll keep spouting them."

His face went suddenly serious. "I mean them, though. In case you had any doubts . . . I mean every word I say to you. The past couple months have been a series of ups and downs for me. They've been mostly ups, really, but I'm feeling a bit lost with myself right now. I'm still floundering around in my life and in my head, but in that diner, I found you, and I can tell that you are worth knowing."

Her heart fluttered. Actually *fluttered* in her chest and made her cough. Though the cough might have been from embarrassment. The rush running through her body was a mix of pleasure and embarrassment. Both feelings could be equally responsible for anything from the odd feeling in her heart, to the cough, to the flush creeping up her neck.

"How was the museum?" she asked, not sure she wanted to acknowledge what he'd said.

"Closed, like you said. And I didn't see anyone on a horse or any model airplanes in the air. And the Wolf People weren't doing tours, so I didn't see any wolves, either. Nice gift shop, though. They seemed like a good cause so I bought a couple stuffed animals to give as baby gifts."

"That's too bad." She didn't know why he would be wandering this part of Idaho, especially when winter was setting in. A good storm would trap him here, in a place where he seemed to have no purpose other than to drive around. "Even if I don't believe you're here to see the sights, I don't want them to be disappointing."

Marc reached out like he was contemplating another piece of pork, then changed his mind. After wiping his fingers on his napkin, he eyed her. "Why do you think I'm here?"

"Drug dealer on the run?" she said, only half joking. "That's the only reason I've been able to come up with that explains someone being up here with no discernable goals and three phones."

He barked with laughter. "Oh man. I wish I'd recorded that."

"Why?" she asked, surprised at how hard he was laughing. Her joke hadn't been that funny.

"I'm sorry. I'm not laughing at your guess." He lifted the back of his hand up to his mouth to slow his chuckles. "Okay, maybe I am laughing at your guess, but that's because my friends will never believe it. I'm not the nerdiest person I know, but only because the competition is steep."

"Then what do you do?" she asked, even more curious now. "Gun runner? Drug dealer? Transporting illegal hamsters? Those are the only reasons I can think for three phones."

"Illegal hamsters," he said, chuckling again and shaking his head. "What kind of TV do you watch?"

"Only the good stuff." She was smiling now, too.

He paused, and she wondered if he wasn't going to tell her what he did, if they would part as unknown to each other as they had been when he'd walked in the door. "Would you believe I developed a texting program for cell phones that sends encrypted texts via SMS and that I just sold it to the largest tech company in the world?"

"That doesn't sound too far from the black market rodent trade," she said as she leaned back in her booth, folded her arms, and evaluated him. He met her comment with his own forthright gaze. It wasn't just the lack of smile on his face that made her realize he was serious, but his eyes were deep and true. If she had sold some tech thing—she had only the shallowest notion of what encryption even meant—to the company she suspected he was referring to, she would be bouncing up and down with joy, possibly even throwing money up in the air for anyone around to catch.

But for all his smiles and flirtations, Marc was made of different stuff. Or maybe such an enormous life change was more profound than Selina could imagine.

"I can pull up the articles on my phone, if you don't believe me," he said, reaching into his back pocket for one of those smartphones he carried. She thought she heard a faint tremble in his voice.

Money was serious business. Having been poor—or nearly so—her entire life, Selina knew that as a truth. But the hitch in Marc's voice wasn't just about the grave implications of money. It seemed important to him that she believed him. Not only because he wanted to be believed and thought of as honest, but the way his eyes focused on her made her think he needed *her* to believe him. The sudden realization made her blink.

"I'd, um, I'd like to see, but not because I don't believe you. I'd like to celebrate your success with you. I'd be *honored* to celebrate your success with you."

Misgivings flashed across his face, but then he pulled out his phones. He must have saved the links to the articles because it only took him three taps on the first phone to bring something up. He handed the phone to her. As she looked down at a *Wall Street Journal* article on the screen, she saw him touching his other phones out of the corner of her eye and setting them faceup on the table.

Selina had believed Marc—she really had—but seeing the article with dollar amounts, pictures, and details had the truth settling itself on her shoulders like a thick wool blanket. It should be comforting, and it definitely brought a warmth to her chest, but too much could feel like a burden.

She set the first phone on the table, and he nudged another one toward her. "I built the platform with a friend," he said. "The money isn't all mine."

The next article was from something called *Information Week.* It had the same general content but with a slightly more techie and less business-related spin, as well as a different picture. The last article was from the *New York Times.* That article was the most detailed, including the sale in a bigger story about mobile security, hacking, and open-source software.

She pushed the two other phones away from her slowly, almost afraid to touch them. "This is a big deal."

One side of his mouth kicked up in a proud smile. "Yeah."

"And not just because of the money."

He shook his head, his smile growing deeper. "The money is nice, but what my buddy and I did was revolutionary. With our competition, you have to have access to a data network to send encrypted texts. Using the actual cell network changes the game completely." Excitement carried his voice a little louder in the last sentence.

"Why are you running away, then?"

"Running away?" Even though he shook his head,

she sensed she'd hit on the truth. "This is my celebratory trip. I'm driving around, seeing the sights, and then I'm going to Snowdance outside of Salt Lake City for a week of skiing. I've booked the best condo they had available, private lessons, and a heli-skiing trip. It will be my first vacation in two years. And when I'm done at Snowdance, I've got a couple other places booked."

She shook her head. "People come to northern Idaho to disappear."

Recognition flickered in his eyes, shuttering the pride on his face. "Maybe that's what I wanted when I planned the trip. No, not *disappear*. But be out of contact with the world for a while. Not have to see a computer screen or check my phone every five seconds."

"You're carrying three phones," she pointed out with a nod at the electronics on the table. "If you want to sever ties, you need to leave them all behind."

"No," he said with a vigorous shake of his head. "I never wanted to sever ties. Put them on hold, maybe, but not sever."

"You've got to leave at least one phone behind if you want to do that," she said with a raise of her brow.

His chuckle was hollow, more than humor. "Setting my life aside for a couple weeks has been . . ." He paused, and his eyes seemed to search the room for the right word. "It has been strange."

"What do you keep checking in on?"

Reservations slipped onto his easy, friendly face. "I've told you a lot about me. What about you? I want to know about you, too."

"What about me? I'm a waitress at a diner in a nothing town, taking one course a semester at the local community college until I can get out. For obvious reasons, your life is more exciting."

"I don't know about that. What are you studying?"

"This semester? I'm taking an art history class."

He gestured his head to her. "I mean, in general. What's your goal?"

The image from her daydream flashed in front of her eyes. She was wearing her fancy black books, a tight black skirt, and black silk top, standing among the colorful artwork of some fabulous new artist that she'd discovered. Then she saw Marc coming in, having passed the gallery and seen her—not the art—in the windows.

She tried to shake the thoughts away. She was too old to have such a silly fantasy, especially since she needed a job that was reliable and paid well. "I'd like to get my nursing degree, but the community college near me doesn't offer the right classes." She paused, trying to figure out how to explain it without sounding like an aimless fool. "Right now, I'm taking classes so I can get some core stuff out of the way and electives that will hopefully transfer. One day, I'll have saved up enough money to be able to move to Spokane and take the rest of the classes I need."

"That sounds interesting. And makes sense." His smile was encouraging, and she felt like she was lying to him.

"Not really. I'm kind of treading water. And to be honest, I feel stuck. Spending money on those classes now means I'm not saving up to move and study somewhere I know the credits will help to get me my degree. But I'm afraid that if I don't take the classes, I'll lose momentum."

Sometimes, momentum was the only thing that kept her going forward.

"Are momentum struggles why you were crying?" he asked gently. "I've been there before."

His confidence was as contagious as his smiles, though for different reasons. Not once had Marc looked at her with pity. To Marc, she was the pretty—though sad—waitress he'd picked up in a diner. And man, it was wonderful to be something so simple.

Everyone in town knew that her stepfather was a waste of space and her mother enabled him. Sometimes when Selina walked through the grocery store, the smiles of the people she saw were less friendly and more indulgent. Anger and apprehension would seethe inside her, boiling and growing until she got home where reality would be lying—drunk—on the couch.

It wasn't enough for Gary to be a drunk. Or to be a letch. Or to be unable to hold a job. But he had to be all three, all at once. Selina had long since stopped trying to figure out why her mom didn't leave the guy. The *why* didn't matter as much as the fact that she wouldn't, and anyway, what did Selina know about long-term relationships and commitment? The only thing she was committed to was getting out of this town and she held tight to that goal, despite the snags life had thrown in her way. *Some day.*

"Ya know, it's a small town, and getting out isn't easy. Poverty, meth, bad schools—take your pick. There's a lot to cry about."

Disappointment darkened his brown eyes. "Come on, now. I mean, it's your life and you can keep it to yourself if you want. But I did share with you."

"Is telling you why I was crying my price for dinner?" Thinking about Gary had put her on edge, and it was reflected in the sharpness of her tone. Worry that her instincts had slipped and that Marc was just a nicer, classier version of Gary snaked through her. Maybe with Marc, when he said something didn't have a price, what he meant was that he hadn't come up with the price yet.

"God, if you have cause to think that about men, I already know why you were crying." The disappointment that had been in his eyes colored to anger, though she knew it wasn't directed at her. "Look, if you don't want to talk about it, that's fine. Tell me what the most interesting thing is that you learned in your art class so far. I want to know that, too."

For the second time that night, she evaluated how genuine he was. And for the second time that night, he looked her straight in her eyes and let her appraise him. She would have expected a man who built security programs to keep information safe, to be closed off and secretive. And maybe most guys like him were. Maybe

Marc normally was, even, but nothing about this interaction was normal.

"My stepfather made a pass at me last night," she admitted, trying not to let her voice waver. He opened his mouth, and she spoke before he could get any words out. "No, that diminishes me and makes what he did seem smaller. Gary often makes passes at me. He likes my looks and my figure. Sometimes he tests my doorknob to see if it's locked. What made last night different was that he was the perfect combination of drunk enough to try to knock down my door and not so drunk that he passed out before he could do it. I spent all night driving around town, just so I didn't have to be at home. And I was crying because I don't know where to sleep tonight."

There was the pitying face she'd been hoping to avoid. Though in Marc's eyes, it was okay. Not great, but bearable. "No friends you can stay with?"

Their conversation paused as the waitress came up to the table and set down their plates. Wood snapped as they both broke their chopsticks apart and the smells of chilies, chicken, and oyster sauce wafted up from the table.

Her belly growled. She'd eaten a small breakfast at Babe's before the restaurant opened, but otherwise that undrunk cup of coffee was the only thing she'd tried to put in her stomach today.

She poked at her food, picking out a piece of red pepper and setting it on her rice. "I've burned through most of my friends' patience staying with them." Sauce glistened on the pepper as she examined it and considered her parents. "I think my mom will actually be worried. She ran away when she was young, got pregnant, and here we are." She dropped the pepper in her mouth.

"You can't move out?"

"Well, now I *can't* go back, not after tonight. But—" she shook her head, knowing that she didn't have any place else to go and so would probably find herself crawling back. Then she swallowed and answered "—Babe barely makes enough to keep that place open, so she can't pay a lot. Plus, anything I make extra goes to paying for college classes and gas and textbooks. And groceries and rent sometimes, and the electric bill." She poked at her food. "You didn't make your escape until you sold your work for millions. I don't need millions, but I need more than a diner waitress's salary."

He looked up from his own plate and met her eyes, his expression serious. "You should come with me." He blinked in evident surprise. "Yeah," he went on after a beat. "Come with me."

Chapter Four

As soon as the words were out of Marc's mouth, he knew it was a good idea. Whatever pleasure he'd gotten driving around the wilds of the Rocky Mountains on his own was long gone now, replaced by nothing but loneliness.

Judging by her narrowed eyes, Selina wasn't quite as thrilled with the idea. "Come *where* with you?"

A piece of hot pepper sailed through the air as his hands opened up in offering, drawing an arc in the air with his chopsticks. "On my adventures!" He was bouncing up and down on the cushion and couldn't stop himself. "If you want, I'll bring you back here after my week skiing at Snowdance is over. Until the first of the year, I don't have anywhere else I have to be."

That was a sad truth.

"Even better," he went on, "maybe you can spend the week I'm skiing looking for a job in Salt Lake. Maybe something that pays better. Maybe a roommate. They have to have a community college there and you could sign up for classes."

A strand of her pale hair fell in front of her eyes,

breaking up the suspicion on her face. "How do you know I'm not crazy?"

"How do you know *I'm* not crazy?" he countered, putting his chopsticks down.

"That was going to be my next question."

He laughed. "That's part of the adventure."

Her head shook quickly, her hair bouncing about her chin. "No. Crazy men in my life are no adventure. One's enough, thank you."

"Do you really wonder if I'm crazy?" he asked, crossing his arms and leaning on the table, leaning in toward her.

"I guess not."

"You guess not?" He chuckled, but her words sliced through him. For all that he sympathized with her distrust, being lumped in with any group that included her stepfather felt like being shoved into a tiny closet filled with people who smell like cat piss.

"Who but a crazy person asks a complete stranger to come with them on a road trip?" she asked.

True, but . . .

"Driving around the country on my own isn't as fun as I hoped it would be."

She blinked. God, when she decided to take a man's measure, that man—at least Marc—felt the need to put his shoulders back and stand as tall as possible. He never wanted Selina to look at him and find him wanting.

"I'll believe that, especially for you. But what if I'm crazy?" She raised an eyebrow. "You haven't answered that yet."

"If you were crazy, I think you would've jumped at the chance."

She actually harrumphed. "What about money? I just said that I don't have any."

"I'm twenty-five and just sold an app for millions of dollars. I'm not asking you for money. I'll already be paying for gas and hotels. You'll be an extra mouth to feed. If you want to pay for your own dinners, you can. But I'm happy to pay for those, too." Her company would be worth the minor additional cost.

"Because you're lonely?" With her brow furrowed, she was the cutest mystified person he'd ever seen.

But *lonely* sounded scarier when she said it. "Well, yes. I'm lonely and need the company. You're trapped and need the escape. We're both getting something from the other."

She narrowed her eyes at him again. "What's the catch?"

"Does there have to be a catch?"

"You just sold your app for millions of dollars and are now wandering around the mountains alone. Sounds to me like there's a catch to everything, even winning the lottery."

Her words felt like someone swatting his nose with a small switch. Sure, it hurt, but more than the pain, what she'd said made his eyes water and he had to refocus on the world around him. "I guess that's true. So then the catch is that you don't know me and I don't know you.

If you say yes and we make horrible traveling companions, then we've both learned a lesson. If that happens, I'll probably be willing to pay to get you away from me. And you'll have to go. That seems like catch enough."

"What about the last of my classes?" She was still protesting, but he could hear how halfhearted they were.

The great idea rushed out of him like a balloon releasing air. "Right. Tests." He'd forgotten about those terrible things, blocked them out of his mind, really, because he'd never been good at taking tests.

"No tests this semester. Just a final paper."

"You can e-mail that, then. I'm sure the professor will take it."

Her mouth twitched. "You seem mighty sure for never having met this professor."

"Do you have good grades already? I mean, if he's pissed that you didn't go to the last couple classes and e-mailed in the final paper, how bad off will you be?"

"Not too bad, I guess. I'm getting an A in the class right now. I probably couldn't get the job, though," she said, more to herself than to Marc.

"What job?" he asked, genuinely curious. It was a good sign for him if she already had a job in mind in Salt Lake.

All the stagnation she felt in her life seemed to come out with her sigh. "My professor has a friend who owns an art gallery. It's silly, but it seems like the coolest job in the world. Not practical and I'd probably starve and be homeless on the salary, but I've always wanted to know what it would be like to work among pretty things."

"You don't know if you don't ask."

"Well, yes, but . . ." In the space between her words, he could hear her deciding to say yes to his plan.

"I'll up the ante." He pushed his hands across the table, palms up, maybe offering her the trip of a lifetime, maybe trying to get her to place her hands in his. He wasn't sure. "If the guy punishes your grade for skipping out at the very end, I'll pay for one of your classes. In Salt Lake City. Here. Wherever you want. That will give you some safety net, at least."

"I'll be leaving Babe in a lurch." Her pitch rose with the last of her objections, and he knew he'd gotten her.

He closed his fists. "She seems to have real affection for you. Do you think she'll be angry?"

"No," Selina said, her *O* long and drawn out.

"Do you want to ask her?"

The more Marc pushed for her to say yes to the idea, the more he wanted it. Not just because he liked to succeed—though he acknowledged that was part of it— but because Selina's company on this trip was one of those ideas that got better the more he thought about it.

Her objections made sense. She might be crazy. He might be crazy. They might end the trip hating each other. But her presence would stop him from thinking about encryption and random session keys and message fragmentation. And he couldn't start a new life if he was mulling over the old one.

At least he didn't think he could. No one seemed to

know what to tell a twenty-five-year-old who had succeeded beyond anyone's wildest dreams but was too young to retire. *Go volunteer with Doctors Without Borders* was all anyone ever suggested, as if they'd never met him at all. He'd been looking for an equivalent Tech Geeks Without Borders, but nothing he'd found had caught his attention.

"I want to talk with her," she finally said. "I should talk with *someone* before I say yes, absolutely. I'd rather talk to her in person, though. This is too complicated to talk about over the phone."

"That's understandable. If you think she's home, we can head over now."

Marc had never had a "real job," and Selina and Babe's bond impressed him. Maybe he was even a little jealous. Working in his underwear in the middle of the night, a pile of orange peels next to him on the desk wasn't a real job in any way his parents understood it.

Once he'd dropped out of college, he'd attached himself to projects he'd found on various technology postings—some aboveboard, some not. The people he'd worked with had been acquaintances, and he had a good network, but he'd never been close with any of them. Except Curtis. He and Curtis had come up with the idea for the encrypted texts, and Marc had thought they were friends, not just geek buddies.

"I'm going to assume Babe will think this is as great of an idea as I do." If he reached out, success—and Selina coming with him—was close enough he might be able to grab ahold of it and kiss it. "Should we find your mom to tell her, too?"

Hesitation pulled at the corners of her eyes. Crap. Saying that had been a bad tack when he was trying to convince her to come.

"Yes," she said and then gnawed on her lip. "But I don't want to tell her in person. She's guaranteed to think this is a bad idea."

"Afraid she'll talk you out of it?" Marc was convinced this idea was great and was certain Babe would see reason, but he didn't believe Selina's mom could even find reason in an empty, well-lit room. Otherwise, she'd have done something to protect her daughter from that awful man she'd married.

"I'm afraid she'll try—or Gary will—and we'll fight."

Right. One of the breadwinners was thinking of driving away in the bread truck, and her stepfather seemed like the type who would respond with abuse toward the nearest woman handy rather than getting his own job. "Should she talk you out of it?"

He wanted Selina to come with him. The trip would be better with her in the car. But he didn't want to be a dick and force her into anything.

Selina gave a vigorous shake of her head. "No. Maybe going with you is a bad idea, but staying here is a bad idea, too. I'll talk to Babe about it, but . . ." She paused, then nodded, apparently at the thoughts in her own head. "But I think I'm coming."

Being the best of two bad ideas pricked his ego, but

quibbling or objecting wouldn't help him win Selina's company.

She waved a hand between them, seeming to dismiss any more objections she wasn't sharing. "I'll call my mom from the road. Babe has a detached garage that I can leave my car in. And if I decide to stay in Salt Lake City at the end of the week, I trust her to sell it for me and send me the money."

"Do you need to go home to pack?" Decision made, Marc's mind moved to the practicalities of this trip.

"No." She looked sheepish for a moment. "When I left last night, I took a backpack I'd already had packed in case I never wanted to go back. And I've had a suitcase in my car for weeks. Gary has been getting more, uh, persistent, and I wanted to be prepared."

That he was *persistent* might be the biggest understatement Marc had ever heard to describe what he didn't want to imagine had been happening in Selina's home.

"Well then," he said, clapping his hands together, "of all the diners in all the towns in all the world, I'm glad I walked in to yours."

"You're cute," she said with a sweet smile, which made his chest swell. If he could keep her smiling with cheesy jokes, they would be A-okay.

He picked up a piece of onion, eager to finish his food and get to Babe's house. His stir-fry had gotten cold, but it tasted better than any food he'd eaten in the last couple of days, including Babe's wonderful pancakes.

"SELINA," BABE SAID, her neutral voice a sure indication that she was worried, "let's go into the kitchen and pack you some food for the car trip."

Selina dutifully stood and followed Babe out of the living room. They hadn't even crossed the threshold into the other room when she whipped her body around. "What are you thinking?" her boss and friend hissed.

Selina glanced over her shoulder to where Marc sat on the floral couch under the painting of a craggy mountain, an icy lake, and the clear blue sky of a perfect Idaho summer day. He had to know that they were talking about him, and he could probably guess that Babe was questioning Selina's judgment. But he wasn't fidgeting and didn't otherwise seem nervous. He was just leaning against the back of the couch, his ankle resting on his knee, looking for all the world like a man at complete ease with himself and his situation.

Confident, which of course he had every right to be. Programming his app had probably been hard, but all the work had paid off. Marc had what Selina wanted: the knowledge that effort toward a goal brought results. Not more treading water.

She wasn't sure where leaving for a spontaneous road trip with a stranger fell in her plans, but it got her out of this town. And that was an accomplishment in and of itself.

She turned back to face Babe's concerned eyes.

"Marc will take me to Salt Lake, and I'll have a place to live for at least a week while I look for work. This isn't how I'd planned to get out of Idaho, but it would be stupid to turn down the opportunity."

Babe blinked several times. "You know nothing about this man. He might be a rapist. Or a murderer. Or worse."

What could be worse than a rapist or a murder? Selina didn't ask. She didn't want to know how Babe would answer.

"Maybe," she said, instead. "But he's who he says is. I've read the news articles, and they're credible sources, too. And I need to be out of town the next time Gary gets drunk enough to forget that he's supposed to be my stepfather."

As she said the words, her palms got clammy and fear pounded in her ears. She'd been afraid of Gary before, but last night was the first time she'd felt honest-to-God terrified. Admitting it to herself didn't calm her body down, but it made her feel better about her decision to run off with Marc. Yes, he was a stranger, and maybe he would snore or his farts would be unbearable, but never once had her gut flickered with fear, especially not for her safety.

Babe cocked her head, her eyes searching Selina's face. "Okay. I know you *need* to be out of that house, and you *want* to be out of this town. Do you have money?"

Selina smiled with relief. "Yes. Some," she corrected.

"I have enough. What's in my savings account right now should pay for rent for a couple months if I don't get a job right away." She was trying not to hang all her hopes on a job at the gallery. Practicality had to trump dreams. "I'll be okay."

Babe's lips thinned. She didn't look as though she thought this was a good idea, but at least she wasn't arguing anymore. "Okay, then. You have my support. I'm not sure this is a good idea, but you're clearly convinced it's not a bad one and that's good enough for me. You've always been a sensible girl. One of my oldest friends lives in Salt Lake, too. If you need help, give her a call."

Selina's heart leaped and bounded with joy before leaning in to Babe and giving her a big hug. "Thank you, thank you, thank you."

Selina hadn't realized how much Babe's approval and encouragement mattered until she was pressed against the woman's soft bosom and wrapped in her tight embrace. Happy tears welled up in her eyes, quickly dampening Babe's shirt.

"Are you crying?" Babe asked. She was sniffling, as well.

"Yes, but I'll be okay. I'll miss you. I'll miss the diner."

"I'll miss you, too." Babe patted her on the back. "Now let's really get some snacks packed for your trip."

They stayed in each other's arms for several long moments, though, with Babe rubbing her hand along

Selina's back. Even though her boss's hair was damp from an earlier shower, Selina could smell the diner grease under the sharp odor of Irish Spring soap. She took a deep breath, trying to memorize the scent, the feel of Babe's arms, and the sound of her breathing. There wasn't much about this place that she would miss, but Babe represented all of it.

SELINA'S SUITCASE WAS heavier than Marc had expected. Having misjudged its weight, he'd had to tug several times to get it out of the trunk. A light snow was starting to fall as he moved his own luggage around in the back of his SUV to make room for Selina's luggage. One flake hit the bull's-eye, slipping down the neck of his jacket and melting between his shoulder blades.

When he turned, Selina was standing behind him, the collar of her coat turned up to protect her neck and her hands clasped in front of her chest. The glow of the streetlight fell in a halo on her head, making her hair look almost white. Snowflakes danced about her, and she looked like a winter angel. Not a fairy, who tricked and played games, but someone who would provide steady comfort at the precise moment he needed it.

Standing next to Selina, Babe didn't look nearly as serene. Selina was looking at him, but Babe was staring at Selina with a mixture of love and worry in her eyes. There were tearstains on both women's cheeks.

Marc slammed the trunk of the SUV, the noise echoing in the cold night air and adding a new finality to their decision. When he turned back, the women were walking toward him. He took a step toward her, which she matched with a large step toward him.

If they could continue to meet each other halfway, they would be okay. No, they'd be better than okay. They would be great. He gave her a reassuring smile, which she returned before turning back to give Babe a hug.

"Bye, my dear," the older woman said, pressing her face into Selina's hair. "Call me if you need anything. I'll drive down to get you if you need me to."

"I won't need," Selina reassured her, which also made Marc feel better. "But I appreciate the offer. Thank you . . . for everything."

Babe patted Selina's face. Tears had returned to both their eyes. Fortunately, Selina's face showed no signs of doubt. If he'd seen any regret on her face, he might have told her that they couldn't do this. But she smiled at him as she pulled away from her friend.

He opened the passenger door for her, and she stepped up, putting her hand on the handle on the inside of the door. "I'll text to let you know our progress. And send you pictures."

The snow had started in earnest now, falling hard enough that it was sticking to Babe's hat and covering the car. Babe nodded. "Do that. I'll worry if I don't hear from you."

"I know." Selina slid into the seat. "I'll miss you."

They both turned their faces to him, like they weren't sure what to do next. He made ending the lingering good-bye easier on both of them by shutting the passenger door.

A scowl scrunched Babe's face. "You take care of her."

"I will." Then he added, "And I won't hurt her."

The older woman rolled her eyes. "Right. That's what all men say. And most of them even mean it."

"Hey," he said, affronted. "You're assuming something more is going to happen on this road trip than what Selina and I talked about."

He had never felt as stupid in his life as he did when Babe raised her eyebrows at him, snowflakes melting on her nose. "She said you were real smart, but now I have my doubts. Selina is cute. You're not so bad yourself. You're both young. You'll be in a car together and then in hotel rooms together. Maybe nothing will happen. But I was young once, too. I remember."

In a flash of insight, Marc saw Babe when she was young, when her face was smoother, her stomach not so generous, and her eyes less wary. He also saw that her remembered youth was both the reason she wasn't trying to talk Selina out of going and the reason she worried about Selina.

"I have no interest in forcing her into anything, if that's what you're implying. As for the rest . . ." His voice trailed off because he had no idea how to finish that sentence with anything remotely truthful. If they did more than talk and share the car, he couldn't promise not to hurt Selina any more than she could promise not to hurt him.

"Well, at least you're smart enough to know your limitations. I'll give you that."

"Thanks."

A couple of years ago, when he was younger and his ego hadn't been battered about by years of near failure designing his app, he would have been insulted by Babe's comment. But he was neither so young nor so stupid. Instead, he saw Babe's protectiveness as confirmation that he'd made the right choice asking Selina to come with him. Babe seemed like the type of person who didn't give her love easily but who loved hard when she did. If Selina had earned that love, then Marc was going to be lucky to have her with him.

"I'll have Selina text you my phone number and any other contact information for me that you'd like. If having my parents' phone numbers will make you feel better, I'll give those to you, too."

"Ha! It would serve you right if I called them and told them what you were doing with a young woman you picked up in a diner." Her face softened, as though Marc had made the first steps to earning her trust. "I want them. I won't call them right away, but don't you doubt that I will if I feel I need to."

He chuckled, nodding his agreement. Babe wasn't making an idle threat. "Then I'll include my grandmother's number, too. She always gives the sternest lectures."

Babe smiled at him for the first time since he and Selina had walked into her living room and told her their plans. She patted him on the arm. "Show her a good time. She needs it," she said, then walked off before he could say good-bye.

As Marc watched her leave, he could feel Selina's gaze through the window behind him. Babe's front door shut, and it was time to go. He walked around the front of the car, opened his door, and climbed in.

"Babe read you the riot act?" Selina asked.

"Yeah," he said, turning the key in the starter. As he shifted into reverse and backed out of Babe's driveway, he was suddenly conscious of Selina's beauty and Babe's certainty that more than driving would be happening on this trip. The possibility was as attractive as the woman sitting next to him, except it also seemed like a terrible idea.

The tires crunched over gravel, ice, and snow as Marc navigated his way to the main road, the sounds filling all the spaces in the Land Rover. He didn't know what to say, and apparently, nor did Selina. Neither of them reached for the radio to drown out the silence, either.

Marc turned onto the highway leading south, their previously easy comradery left behind in Babe's driveway.

Chapter Five

SELINA WOKE TO the car slowing down. She stretched her arms above her head, then looked around, expecting to see a gas station, or motel, or something other than snow and the side of the road as the SUV came to a stop.

"Where are we?" she asked.

"Honestly? I don't know." Marc shook his head, a slow, deliberate motion that worried Selina more than the blinding white their headlights lit up in front of them.

He cocked his head toward her, his brows raised and worry making the wrinkles of his expression especially shadowed in the dark of the car. "You wouldn't happen to be able to look around and tell, would you?"

She peered past the heavy falling snow into the blackness beyond. Mountains had to be within spitting distance of the road, but she couldn't see them for all the snow in the night. She couldn't see anything more than a couple of feet from the car, even out the windshield where the headlights should have helped.

She turned to him and cringed. "Idaho?"

"Yeah," he said with a wry chuckle. "I hope so. The road has been so hard to follow for the past hour that I'm not even sure about that."

As she looked back outside, cold started to seep into her bones. Marc hadn't turned the car off yet, so it wasn't the actual cold from the outside. It was fear. "Are we going to keep going?"

Did I misjudge you?

She couldn't ask him that, though. And she didn't feel that this was the moment when he'd change from the nice, funny, flirtatious guy in the diner to a scary man who would kill her and leave her body in the wilderness.

But that didn't mean she didn't think it. There had been enough news stories about missing young women that she knew it was possible, that her gut feelings could have failed her. And Gary was a perfect example of how men could be rotten in many different ways.

He shook his head. "I'm not comfortable driving with this little visibility. If you think you can do it, I'll give you the keys. I don't want to spend the night in the car, and I especially don't want to have to dig us out in the morning."

His words reassured her fears. It wasn't even so much what he said but how he said it, calm and even, as though he didn't have any reason not to trust her with his life. Because that's what he was doing when offering to let her drive. He was trusting her with his life as much as she had trusted him with hers when she'd agreed to accompany him on this journey.

"No," she said, trying to find the space between the flakes where the road might be. Or the skeletons of tall grasses. Or anything that might hint to her where the road was and where it was not. "I've driven in bad weather before, but this is beyond anything I'm comfortable with, too."

"I passed a couple stopped cars down the road. I don't think we're the only ones caught in the storm." The words came out of his mouth as more breath than sound, and she realized that he'd been frightened when driving, far more frightened than she had realized by just looking at him.

What else happened in his mind that his placid, friendly face covered up? A lot, she guessed. He looked on the geeky side, what with ears and nose and brows all too big for his face. But geeky looks and intelligence didn't translate into creating and selling multimillion-dollar technology. That kind of work took tenacity, dedication, and force of will. A person didn't stumble over that kind of success overnight.

If she wanted to understand him better, she'd have to watch him more carefully. And, she considered as she switched her gaze from his face to the weather outside and back to his face, she wanted to watch him more carefully.

"So what should we do now?" she asked. "Is there a town close enough that we can turn back?"

"I'm not sure." Marc turned the car off. "I'm sorry. I

put our lives at risk because I had a destination, and I was determined to push us until we got there rather than stop for the night when the storm kicked up. I would never have been able to forgive myself if something had happened to you."

"Babe would hunt you down," she said. Her mom would be sad, too. Selina wasn't so disappointed in her mom that she didn't know the woman cared for her.

Being farther away—even just a two- or three-hour drive—from her mom and Gary, the sadness that had had her crying at the diner had lessened like the sky brightening after a heavy rain. The clouds were still oppressive, but there was enough sun trying to bust through that she could see shadows.

Plus, she had Babe. And many trapped people didn't even have a Babe.

"So I guess we're spending the night in the car?" She'd known they would be in the car together for long periods of time, but overnight hadn't occurred to her.

He frowned. "If neither of us are comfortable driving in this, I don't have a better idea."

The car's engine was still hot so the snow was melting and sliding off the front of the car, but the side mirrors had gotten cold quickly and the white was starting to accumulate on the dark metal. Being closed in the car all night would be tight and cold, but being outside in a tent—which they didn't have anyway—would be worse.

"How are we going to keep warm?" She was sure he

had a plan—he seemed like the kind of guy who had plans—but hearing him say the words would be reassuring.

"I've got my ski clothes, which should be plenty warm, and a couple emergency blankets in the back. Um . . ."

She knew immediately by the side-glance he gave her what he was going to say, and that she wouldn't like it.

"People, uh, also cuddle for warmth. Wait—" he waved a frantic pause "—*huddle* is the word I want. *Huddle* is better."

She pursed her lips at him, amused and half pretending not to be. "Was that slip on purpose?"

"Scout's honor," he said, holding up a hand in a three-finger salute. Even the dark, snowy night wasn't able to hide the twinkle in his eyes. "I promised, and I keep my promises."

She believed him instantly. In the conflict rushing through his eyes like waves through a narrow channel, she saw the same conflict she was feeling. She disliked the idea of huddling with Marc in the backseat of the SUV much less than she had expected.

Instead of trying to figure out how they could be close and warm without risking hands accidently brushing hands and crotches, she wondered how his arms would feel wrapped around her and if he used any cologne that might be lingering on his skin.

"Huddle," she confirmed, trying to push those thoughts out of her mind. "Yes. Okay. I have some warm clothes, too, and a pair of wool socks. Maybe we can stuff a bag for a pillow?"

"That's a good idea." He was speaking as slowly as she was, as if he was also trying to wrap his mind around the reality of the tight space and close bodies without seeming like he was actually interested in it.

"Should we get out and get the stuff?" she asked, gesturing toward the back of the car with her head.

"No. I don't want to open the door and let the warmth out any more than we have to. Think you can crawl over the center console? We can reach the luggage from the backseat. The bench seat will be more comfortable for sleeping anyway."

"Mmhmm." She nodded. Their conversation felt more like a dance than a chat. And not a fun dance but like passing an ex you still have feelings for in a tight aisle in the grocery store. Heart rushing, throat a little tight, but taking careful steps—and even more careful words—so you don't end up stepping as close to them as you want to or risk giving away your interest.

Tagging along with a stranger on his personal exploration journey could only work if they didn't have sex. Sex would complicate her already-complicated free hotel rooms and subsidized food. There was a difference between running away in the company of a stranger and running away *with* a stranger. The latter was much messier.

Struggling *not* to have sex with the way she was starting to want him would be almost as problematic, though.

"You go first," she said.

"All right." He crawled and pushed and groaned as he fit his large body through the small space between the front seats.

His contortions meant she had an up close and personal view of a fine ass in old, worn jeans. She blinked. Her new knowledge of his body was inescapable, but she didn't have to keep it at the front of her mind where she would see it every time she closed her eyes. She could push it to the back of her head.

She could.

Even when she was curled up next to him—*huddled* for warmth, she corrected herself—for the entire night.

"Your turn," he said, a hand outstretched.

The tips of his fingers were cold as she slid her hand into his. Then his hand closed around hers and the heat of his body shot through her, making her weak in the knees and confusing everything she'd just promised herself about sex, and forgetting, and complications. She peered over the center console, but by the time she could see his face, he'd hidden his reaction to the touch. If he'd had one in the first place, that was. There was always the possibility that she was imagining the furtive glances and curious eyes.

God, Selina. You meet one nice guy and all you can think about is . . .

Well, what was she thinking about? Sex? A quick fling bound to end when they parted in a couple of weeks? More? And what was *more*?

She pushed off with her foot, whacking her head on the ceiling of the SUV in the process. She overcorrected her climb, shifted her weight, and fell right into Marc's lap.

"Ouch," she cried out, rubbing the top of her head.

"Are you okay?" His arms were wrapped around her, catching her and holding her against him.

"Yes." When she shifted, his arms popped away from around her, as if they had been a rubber band stretched too tightly and suddenly cut. She scrambled away from him in the tight space until she was at the other end of the bench seat. They were as far from each other as possible in such small confines. Hers wasn't the only breath coming in a little fast and heavy, she realized. And she wasn't stupid enough to think her racing heart was the exertion of getting into the backseat. Not when she could trace where Marc's arms had been around her.

"So," she said with a clap of her hands. "Let's figure out our bedding and get settled. It's getting late."

"Right."

With some minor movements, he was able to get to his knees, and there was his nice butt again. It was dark, but that didn't mean there wasn't enough light to see—and to appreciate—what was there.

Zippers rasped, and Marc rustled through his luggage. Soft pieces of clothing hit Selina's shoulder as he yanked them out. She pulled a couple of heavy coats, his emergency blanket, and ski pants to the middle seat. He collapsed back on his butt, his fist full of ski caps, scarves, and two pairs of gloves.

"There," he said, triumphantly setting the rest of the warm clothing on the seat between them. He grabbed one of the ski coats and shoved his arms through it. "I hate to let any warm air out, but I need to pee. At least you'll get privacy to change. Take whatever of the clothing you want. I'll use the rest."

"Okay. Thanks."

He nodded, then cold air rushed into the car and Marc stepped out. For the brief moment that the door was open, she heard nothing. The snow was already deep enough that it muffled even the sound of itself falling. There was no wind, no cars, no squawks of owls. Without Marc's comforting presence to keep it at bay, the oppressive weight of desolation oozed down the sides of the car, inflating like a balloon into the empty space. Selina took a couple of deep breaths to remind herself that she was free, then focused on her task, sorting through the items Marc had pulled from the back.

She shucked her jeans in favor of a pair of too-big ski pants and put some ski socks over her own. His puffy down coat looked more comfortable to sleep in—and warmer—than her structured winter coat, so she put that on, completing the whole look with a University of Washington knit cap topped with a purple pom-pom and a pair of black mittens.

The door opened and Marc climbed back into the car, bringing another blast of cold air with him.

"My turn," she said, reaching into her purse and grabbing a pack of tissues before she could think too much about how cold the air would be on her bare ass and how much she'd have to struggle with the layers to get her ass bare in the first place.

When she returned from outside, Marc had scrunched up some clothes into a softer duffel and set it on one end of the bench seat. She climbed in, and for a few seconds, they stared alternately at each other and at the narrow space of the seat. Then he shrugged and scooted around until he was lying on his side, his back against the back of the seats and arms open for her to spoon with him. Pushing down her competing hesitation and desire, she crawled next to him, fitting her butt against his crotch and her head so that his arm was under her neck. To seal the deal, she pulled the small blanket over them.

"Well." His breath danced across the back of her neck as he whispered the word. His mouth must be right above her ear. Maybe if he pursed his lips and leaned a little forward, he could nibble on her ear.

She liked when men nibbled on her ear . . .

"This is tight, but it's not too bad," he said. "Think we can last the night?"

Between the awkward pillow and his arm, her neck was turned at a strange angle and she'd have the mother of all cricks in the morning. His legs were too long for the seat, and he'd compensated by draping one leg over her. She was completely cocooned in him.

Breathing deeply, she waited for the moment of panic to strike. The moment when she felt trapped, worried that he would take advantage of her, that she wouldn't be able to escape or stop him. But the moment never came. Her breath slowed without her even trying to force it. She wasn't exactly comfortable, but she was warm and safe, which was more than she'd felt in months.

"This will be great," she said, closing her eyes. "Good night. And thank you."

MARC WOKE UP with an erection. And not regular morning wood, either. His face was full of the floral smell of a woman's hair and his arms were hugging a soft, curvy body. He was warm. Hot, even, which he hadn't expected, but the ski clothing, blanket, seats, and Selina's body were providing more than enough heat to combat the cold. Even his face, which was buried in Selina's neck, was warm. He lifted his head to get her hair out of his nose before he sneezed and woke her.

Sunlight beamed in through the back windows, glinting off Selina's pale hair. He propped himself up on his elbow so that he could get a look at her. Her face, which had been tight even when she was laughing, had relaxed in sleep. Her jaw was soft, and if he wasn't mistaken, she was snoring quietly.

She was so beautiful. He'd already liked the look of

her when she was sour and serving him breakfast, but the pretty waitress was no comparison to the sleeping woman. This was what she was supposed to look like when she wasn't worried about her physical safety, or money, or where she was going to sleep at night.

He noticed the moment she woke up because her eyelids fluttered. And then she stiffened. His erection hadn't gotten any less prominent while he'd been admiring the way her lashes fell on her cheeks.

"You warm enough?" he asked, deciding that the best course of action was to pretend he wasn't sporting a boner. He didn't think she was actually afraid of him, but she was skittish and, from what she'd told him of her home life, she had good reason to be.

"Overly so."

At least she wasn't rushing to get away from him. And she wasn't moving his top arm away, so he kept it— and the leg he had draped over her—right where they were.

"Sleep okay?"

Her mouth curved into a slight smile. "Yeah. Once I fell asleep, I slept like a rock."

"It's sunny," he said stupidly. "The storm has passed."

She laughed, blinking. "I can see that."

Her stomach growled. "I wonder where the nearest coffee and donuts are. Where are we?"

"Still don't know." He shifted as well as he could, stretching his arm out in front of them. Scooting to straighten out his knees, he bumped her forward a bit. "Sorry."

"No, it's okay. I should move. I'm pretty sure my foot is asleep. Or it ran away in the middle of the night. One of the two. And I need to pee."

"Right." He held on to her until the count of ten, then opened his arms and she climbed to sitting up as best as she could.

The side of her face that had been resting on the duffel had a massive, deep wrinkle running across her cheek from her ear to the corner of her mouth. She had sleep in the corners of both eyes and a little mark of white drool that met up with the wrinkle. She looked like she had slept well, and he was sure he didn't look much better. After a good night's sleep his hair usually looked like loosened coils of brown yarn.

At least it distracted from the morning breath that had him wanting to smack his mouth.

She grabbed for her pack of tissues, then looked back at him, her hand on the door handle. "Um, it's light out. Please don't look."

"I won't. But do a little scoping while you're out there, would ya? I want to make sure we're still on the road and not snowed in. There's a shovel in the back, though if you need to dig to find it, we'll both be sorry."

While she was outside, he had the chance to smack the staleness of sleep out his mouth in private and dig in his center console for some mints.

"It's not so bad out there," she said, climbing into

the car. "It must have stopped snowing soon after we stopped. The tire tracks are easy to see, and we should be able to get out no problem." She patted his leg. "From what I could tell, you even stayed on the road up until you pulled over."

Her touch zinged up his body, rushing into his ears and tingling the tips of his fingers.

Fuck. He'd promised her that the trip had no cost, that there were no expectations, and he'd meant it. He still meant it. He was a man, not a bull. But not thinking about what she would feel like if they were so close had been easier before she'd been curled up in his arms, before his erection, and before she'd touched his leg of her own accord.

They'd have to get double beds in each hotel room. He would have asked for them anyway, but now it was sleep in separate beds or he'd be on the floor. Or he'd have to pull the old fairy tale trick and sleep with a sword between them. He didn't want her to wake up with an erection pressing against her again.

"Well good," he said, plastering a wide, innocent smile on his face. "I figure we can drive for five hours or so, then see what's interesting wherever we stop. In the meantime, it's my turn for a trip to our expansive bathroom."

Her smile was big, honest, and without hesitation. "It is certainly the largest bathroom I've ever used, and I do like the white."

The sun was warming the air up fast and was almost

blinding as it reflected off the snow. He took care of his business, inspected his path back onto the highway, then climbed into the driver's seat and grabbed his phone to check his messages. The first one was from Curtis, assuring him again that they didn't need to talk. He frowned.

The second message was from one of the guys in charge of the project that Marc's baby had become. The e-mail had a veneer of politeness, but the words didn't cover up the point the man was trying to make. In sum, *Leave us alone. We're fine. You sold the project and declined further participation.*

Or as Marc would put it, *Fuck off.*

The e-mail from Curtis hurt worse than the dismissive e-mail from a stranger, though. Terry was *his*, as much as it was Curtis's, and brushing him off was a real shit thing to do.

You gave Terry up before Curtis brushed you off.

He tossed his phone into the console and twisted the key in the starter. A small, petty part of him was grateful that he hadn't bought one of those cars with the push-button starter; it wouldn't have been nearly as satisfying. What he really needed was a motorcycle with no muffler to drown out the voice of reason.

"Something wrong?" Selina's voice beside him was soft with concern.

"No," he growled, then felt bad when she just blinked and said, "Okay," in a small voice.

"Yes," he said. The word came out in a huff, much

like an upset, petulant dog's would. He shifted in his seat so that he was talking to her face rather than the steering wheel. "I sold my app. It was my baby. Curtis and I worked on it for *years.* We did side programming jobs for money, but we spent all our spare time on this thing. No vacation. No sick days."

He swiped his hand down his face, rubbing at the memories of being wrapped in a blanket, a bucket next to him on the floor, and a bottle of ginger ale on the desk next to his computer. He'd written the backbone of some beautiful code that day between bouts of being sick in the bucket.

She put her hand on his knee. Two touches, but he was too worked up to appreciate this one. "You mentioned that at the Chinese restaurant. I can't imagine putting in that kind of work for anything. I don't even know what coding is, really. I was really impressed. Still am."

"But there's more we can do," he said, unable to keep the whine from his voice.

"A flaw?" she asked.

"Well," he hedged, "not a flaw exactly. I mean, it's not going to break. And it works. But it's cumbersome. I've thought of a way to bypass the biggest issue standing between us and wider adoption of the product by the general public."

And now that he'd figured it out, that fix was all he could think about.

"And you've told Curtis?"

He gestured to the phone. "Curtis and some other people. I haven't told them what the fix is. I just want a meeting to talk with them about it."

Her mouth twitched. "Do you miss working on the project?"

"Oh God, yes." He banged the back of his head against the headrest. "Selling the project was exciting, and I learned all sorts of things about the business of computers. I thought I'd sell the program and be done with it. That having all this money and free time would be liberating." The reality of his situation was as blinding as the sun off the snow. "But it's not. It's very boring."

"Why don't you work on something else?"

"Oh, I will." He waved his hand. "I've got all sorts of ideas about things I want to do."

He did. Or, at least, he had until he'd gotten in this stupid SUV and driven into the mountains to find himself like he was some kind of hippie rather than a nerd who used to retreat from the sun like a vampire.

"But first I've got to get this solution implemented. Then I can move on to something else."

She bit her lip.

"What?" he asked. It looked like, if she wasn't careful, she might choke on the words she was obviously holding back.

"I don't know you very well . . ."

He raised an eyebrow. This was not the start of anything good. Like, *It's not you, it's me,* when it was really about the way you took your coffee black, or didn't eat eggs, or didn't like cats. "But . . . ?" he said, drawing out the word in invitation.

"Have you considered that you're stuck on this old thing because you succeeded at it and it's scary to start something new that might not be nearly such a success? Sophomore efforts and all that."

Her words pushed him against the back of his seat as if she'd shot an arrow—bull's-eye—straight through his chest, pinning him. She couldn't be right, could she? He had all kinds of ideas about what he wanted to work on next. Lists and lists and lists of them. Plus, all those people who wouldn't give him work or answer his calls a couple of years ago were now coming to him with job offers. If he couldn't focus on any of the ideas on any of those lists and hadn't e-mailed or called any of those companies back yet, it was because he wanted the time to think. Not because he was *afraid*.

"It's a valid question, but that's not what is happening in this case. After I get this fix checked out, I'll move on to something new. I've got companies contacting me all the time, as well as independent guys looking to do something just as cool."

She nodded, but he could tell that she didn't really believe him.

The heat from the engine had melted all the snow that had accumulated on the hood of the car, and water was now dripping down the windshield. He turned on the wipers to clear his view, then shifted the car into drive and eased his foot off the brake. The tires caught traction pretty easily and were able to inch forward until they were on the road, which had already been salted. Apparently they'd both slept through the salt trucks, and if they'd kept sleeping much longer, they probably would have been woken up by the Idaho Highway Patrol knocking on the window.

As soon as he was comfortable with the car on the road and as certain as he could be that they weren't going to slide off into the ditch—or off a cliff—Marc took his hand off the wheel and put his palm on Selina's leg. He wanted to feel that she was there, solid and breathing next to him, especially because he wasn't sure what else in his life was constant. She may not be here forever, but she was here now. And now was what he needed.

She stared at the touch but didn't push his hand off the way he had worried she would. To his surprise, after initially tensing, the muscles under his hand relaxed.

"I'm glad that you're impressed with me and my work," he said. "It's an easy thing to be impressed by, I guess. But I'm impressed by you, too. You're working, and going to school, and have a shitty home life, and you don't trust that you'll be able to sleep safely. Yet you're still getting good grades, making money, and pushing on."

She placed a hand on top of his and gave him a gentle squeeze.

"Big, splashy things like selling a product for millions of dollars in your twenties is what makes the news," he continued. "But pushing forward in life while everything seems to be against you is the kind of grit that makes the world function. And if no one's told you lately, I think you're great."

When he glanced at her face, he noticed dampness in her eyes. "No one's told me that in a long time. Thank you."

Chapter Six

"HAVE YOU CALLED your mom yet?" Marc asked Selina about two hours into their drive.

"No," she said, keeping her eyes forward.

"Didn't you say you were going to as soon as we hit the road?" He hadn't mentioned it last night because she'd fallen asleep almost immediately on the drive. And she had obviously needed it. But no matter Selina's relationship with Gary, her mom probably needed a phone call as much as Selina had needed the sleep.

"I know. I wanted to," Selina answered, though she made no move to reach for her phone.

"So why don't you?"

She shrugged like a moody child.

The SUV rolled along the highway, between hills of snow with dead grass poking out of the white depths, occasionally meandering through places with rock faces on either side where it had been cheaper to cut through the rock than it had been to build the road around them.

Just as Marc was giving up on Selina answering, she spoke in a small voice. "What if she didn't notice I was gone?"

Everything in the world seemed to slow down as he considered what it would be like to wonder that about your mother. Then he saw that he had lessened the pressure of his foot on the gas and they had actually slowed down. He hit the pedal a little harder, getting them back up to speed. Then, trying to concentrate on driving at least as much as he was concentrating on listening to Selina, he asked, "Why wouldn't she notice you were gone?"

"She didn't call me last night. She's never called me any of the times I didn't go home because I knew Gary would be there." Her voice was still small, but anger rasped at the edges.

She was trying to see if her mom noticed and cared about her. That was understandable, if heartbreaking. "Are you going to just wait for her to call you?"

Selina shrugged, looking out the window. He couldn't see what her eyes were focused on, but the view out the passenger window was no different than the view out his window. As far as he could tell, she was staring out into space. "It would be nice if she called me once."

He paused a beat before saying anything else. "I have a pretty good relationship with my parents, I guess," he told her. "We have a better relationship than most of my friends do with their parents, at least. But I know I can't expect out of them what I'm not willing to do myself."

"Thank you, Dear Abby," she said.

He frowned. "Sarcasm is not attractive."

She turned away from the window long enough to

give him a scornful look. "You just said that you have a better relationship with your parents than most of your friends do. When you've met Gary at his worst, then you can lecture me about how I should reach out to my mother."

He opened his mouth to argue his point, then stopped himself so that he could process what she'd said. Maturity and taking a step back had served him well in the past. They would serve him well again.

"You're right. Your home life sounds miserable. And I'm amazed that you are as put together as you are. I shouldn't judge."

"Thank you," she said, turning back to stare out the window.

"But you did say that you would call her." He struggled to make his tone nonjudgmental and supportive, even though disappointment surged through his body. Granted, he didn't know Selina that well, but she hadn't seemed like a coward. "So when do you plan to do that?"

"Today."

"That didn't sound very confident."

"You're talking to me as if I'm a child," she snapped. "You're only a couple years older than I am."

He risked a quick glance at her. Her lips were pursed, and her face was set in the same scowl he remembered from breakfast at the diner. God, that had only been a little over twenty-four hours ago. Had he really only known Selina for such a short amount of time? If he let his mind go blank, he could still remember what she felt like in his arms, as if she had been there before and should be there again. He also remembered that her expression at the diner hadn't been a bad mood so much as it had been physical and emotional exhaustion. One uncomfortable night's sleep in the back of a car wasn't going to change that. He had more empathy than this; he just had to use it.

He took a deep breath and put his hand on her knee. "What would Babe tell you to do?"

That won him another look from her, this time with her brows lifted up to her hairline. "Have you called your parents to tell them where you are and that you picked up a stranger to take with you on your little vacation?"

He could feel the hammer hit the nail with that one, though he said, "Those situations are completely different."

"How?"

"Well . . ." His mind raced over all the differences, put them in order of importance, numbered them, and weighed which ones he should explain first. Then he stopped himself from lecturing. She was right. Not that their situations were different, but that his parents would want to know that he wasn't driving alone. And they would be very interested to know he'd picked up a girl.

"You're right. I should call my parents. A bargain, then. When we stop for dinner, I'll call my parents and you call yours. Deal?"

She sighed. "Can I think about it?"

"Sure. We've got a lot of time before dinner."

She nodded, either to his comment or in agreement about calling, he wasn't sure. And he certainly wasn't going to ask right now. Instead, he took a look at the road signs and tried to guesstimate where they would be in a few more hours of driving.

"So about sights for today," he started. "I think there's a birds of prey habitat somewhere along this highway and, if my memory serves me, something called Craters of the Moon."

When she looked over at him this time, she gave him a slight smile that looked more like relief at his change of topic than anything else. "I don't know what there is to see at Craters of the Moon in winter, so how about the bird thing?"

"Bird thing it is," he said with a nod.

He snuck another glance at her. She still looked tired, but there was a resignation on her face that made him think she was glad he had maneuvered her in the right direction when it came to her mom. One squeeze of her knee and a corresponding pat of her hand on his, and he turned his attention back to the drive.

THE COLD IDAHO wind was blowing extra hard as they climbed out of the car at the overlook. Selina pulled her coat tighter around her body, grabbing on to the collar and hiking it up to cover as much of her ears as possible.

"Cold?" Marc asked. He was swinging his arms as

though he didn't have a care in the world, but Selina suspected it was partly because *he* was cold. His face was bright with excitement, though, and his enthusiasm was contagious.

She smiled in response. "A little, but the walk will do me some good."

"Come on, then," he said, clapping his hands together. "I've been driving around to see stuff, and so far almost everything has been closed. I'm just happy this is open."

Gravel crunched under her boots as she walked behind him on the trail to the canyon edge. The snowstorm had left only a dusting of snow on the high plateau of the canyon. With the sun bouncing off the white surfaces, all the colors around her seemed more vibrant. The blue of the sky was brighter, the black and gray of the rocks were deeper, and even the tan of the dead grass looked more alive.

Or maybe, Selina thought as she sidled up to Marc who had stopped to read a sign, what she was seeing was a reflection of her own happiness. Her entire body felt lighter. Her *soul* felt lighter. Light enough that she could take a running start, open up her arms, leap off the canyon, and fly.

Most of her joy was related to the fact that she finally had gotten out of Athol and was pursuing her own dreams, but some of it was the man next to her. Though being prodded in the car about calling her mom had been annoying, she was glad he'd done it. She'd needed the push, but she'd also needed him to back off. He seemed to know instinctively when to do one and when to do the other.

Selina admired the view around them. The landscape seemed to go on forever. Birds cried and chirped in the air, and the wind picked up Marc's floppy hair, lifting parts of it until it was almost standing straight up.

He smiled, taking one step closer to her until their shoulders were nearly touching. "Have you ever been here before?"

"No." Though, right now, she couldn't think of any place she'd rather be.

"Cool, huh?" He held out a hand. "Come on. Let's finish walking to the overlook."

She didn't take his hand, even though she wanted to. And to her relief, he didn't seem to be offended or disappointed.

"God, this is amazing," he said when she caught up with him at the overlook.

Walking up to the rim made her heart race. Black rock jutted out from the sides of the canyon, obscuring the view of the river in places, which snaked hundreds of feet below them. Then there was a harsh cry—seemingly out of nowhere—and a large bird flew directly overhead before plunging into the canyon.

"Holy shit," Marc said as they both jumped back. "What kind of bird was that?"

"I don't know," she answered, her tone echoing the amazement in his. "I didn't read the sign that closely."

She'd been too busy looking at the landscape and Marc.

"I did." He shook his head. "And I still don't know what the bird is. Big. And I think maybe a bird of prey."

She smirked and raised a brow at him. "Well, this *is* a refuge for birds of prey."

His laugh at her smart remark rang delightfully in her ears. "Since neither of us remember what the birds are, we can give them our own names. Big for that bird was an understatement. And it was brown, I think. So I name it . . . Big Brown Bird."

"That's . . ." She was about to say *a stupid name* when she turned to look at him and saw the mischievous glint in his eyes. "We can do better than that."

He gave an easy shrug. "Well, Terry is the encrypted texting app Curtis and I developed. My phones are Veronica, Megan, and Holly. It seems I name things after women, so if I name the bird, I'm going to assume it's female. Hope that's okay by you." He smirked again.

"Why do you do that?"

He cocked his head. "Name things?"

"Name things female names."

"The tech industry is a bit of a boy's club. It's nice to have women around, however they come along."

His explanation made some sense, but there was a better way to address that issue. "You could make a point to hire women."

His amused face fell into seriousness. "I could have, I guess, if I'd taken the offer to stay on with Terry after the sale."

"A goal for the future," she offered.

"Whatever mine might be." Behind the lightness in his voice was a slight tinge of loss and emptiness. A restlessness that his winter of travel and leisure wouldn't fill.

She took a couple of steps closer to him. He stretched out an arm, and she slipped in even closer to him. He was a buffer against the wind. That was the lie she told herself as his hand rested on her shoulder and she leaned her head against him.

A night spent cuddling on the back seat of his SUV. The touch of his hand on her knee. The solid, comforting weight of him next to her. None of these moments came without cost, she knew. She enjoyed his touch too much. She'd had boyfriends, but she hadn't felt as comfortable with any of them after three months as she did with Marc after less than twenty-four hours.

But they would get to Salt Lake City and go their separate ways—Marc to his travels, and Selina to her new life. One that, if she was lucky, would include a job surrounded by beautiful things in a world she couldn't have imagined living in Athol.

Marc wasn't to be relied on. She was not going to repeat her mother's mistakes.

A gust of wind whipped past them and she leaned closer to him.

"We should assume the bird's a woman," she said, returning to the lighter conversation. "And name it something majestic. Like after a goddess or a queen."

"Elizabeth," he offered. "Both generations of queens are impressive."

"I was going to say Cleopatra, but I like your suggestion better. Less tragic." Right now, focusing on strong women who lived long, successful, independent lives seemed like a better talisman than a queen who'd committed suicide.

A flock of birds passed below them, darting and dancing about the cliffs of the canyon edge.

"What shall we name them?" she asked with a nod of her head.

"Pleiades, I think. The seven sisters who were turned first into doves and then into stars."

She liked that. As she watched the birds, their freedom made her heart sing. She had that freedom now, too, thanks to Marc. She only needed to use it wisely.

Wisely could include flirting, though, couldn't it?

"Those aren't doves," she said with a gentle nudge.

"Oh?" His voice rose, amused and teasing. "Did you read the sign?"

"Well, no."

He nodded. "Precisely. My limited expertise says doves, if only because it fits better with the name I gave them."

His rationale was silly and made no sense at all, but it made her laugh. "You can insist that they are doves when we see a . . ." She tried to think of a bird as unexpected as a dove in this sparse landscape. "A heron," she said, finally.

At that moment, a great blue heron flew past them, its head tucked back against its body and its neck curved into an *S*.

They both stood stunned for a moment, then laughed, holding on to each other for support. When Selina finally caught her breath, she said, "That'll teach me to make predictions."

"When I left for this trip," he said, his voice deep and serious. "I never could have predicted this. Or you."

She wondered if he was going to acknowledge the connection between them, but his voice turned light again. "Well, Selina, you summoned the heron, so I think you should get to name her."

"Cindy Lauper," she said, with a firm nod.

"Why?" He sounded genuinely surprised.

"Because I can't imagine a heron named Cindy Lauper. So many things I couldn't have imagined have happened in the past twenty-four hours. Why not that one?"

"That reasoning is as sound as any I've given for any of my names," he said with a chuckle.

They stood like that at the edge of the canyon, his arm wrapped around her, naming birds after famous— and infamous—women until their cheeks were red from the cold and the wind, and their teeth were chattering.

Their hands brushed several times as they walked the short path back to the car, but she never slipped her hand into his and he never grasped on to hers. Like the bird that had surprised them from the sky, their relationship would soon be out of sight. If she tried to hold on to it, she would only get hurt.

IT WAS GETTING dark when they drove into Jerome, Idaho, a small town on the edge of Snake River Canyon. Marc turned at the signs for a hotel and pulled around to the front door. As soon as he got out of the car, Selina pulled out her phone to call her mom. To her surprise, her mom picked up on the first ring.

"Selina? Is that you? What happened? You haven't come home in days! And I didn't know where you were. Usually I, at least, know where you are."

The worry in her mom's voice made Selina choke on sadness she hadn't realized was going to crop up. Not regret—everything about the drive convinced her that she'd made the right decision—but sorrow that driving away with a nice stranger still seemed like the smart thing to do.

"I've decided to move to Salt Lake City."

"I didn't even know you were thinking about moving." Confusion stilted her mom's words. "I mean, I know you talked about moving out, but I thought to Lewiston or Coeur d'Alene. Spokane, maybe, if you were moving to another state."

"The opportunity to move to Salt Lake came up last night, and it was too good to refuse. I have a place to stay for a week or so while I look for a job and a free ride down here. I can make it work." She tried for as chipper a voice as she could find to make the whole idea sound like a well thought-out one, rather than the last-minute, half-panicked decision it had been.

"There's a man involved, isn't there?" Now that her mother's concern had worn off, scorn had set in.

"Of course there is." Selina ignored her mom's implication, trying instead to steer the conversation to the real issue. Or at least the heart of the real issue. "I've been telling you for a long time that Gary made me uncomfortable. And he finally went too far."

Her mom didn't say a word. Selina couldn't even hear her breathing. Cars raced by on the busy road outside the hotel, and the traffic from the highway was audible, too.

"There's another man," her mother snarled. "This isn't just because of what you say about Gary."

"A man came into the diner, yes," she confirmed. "He was going to Salt Lake City and offered me a ride. He's nice, but it's not what you think."

"He's gay?"

The feeling of Marc's erection pressed against her in the morning flashed through her mind. Maybe it was the normal erection men get in the morning, but Selina knew her presence had probably had something to do with it also.

She picked up a gum wrapper, balled it up, then tossed it to the floor. "No. He's not gay."

"Are you pregnant?"

Selina coughed, choking down the retort that she wasn't her mother and wouldn't make the same mistakes. She'd made different ones, which had been enough. "No." Her voice was short and stiff.

"You know, if you run away with a man, he'll never recognize your independence."

Selina cut her mom off before she could get too far into her story. "I know, Mom. I know what mistakes you made and what you regret." Her mom had never actually said she regretted having Selina, but regretting the man and the move was close enough. "I can fancy it up any way I want: I know I'm running away. I know you ran away and look where it got you. But things will be different for me."

Marc was exiting the lobby of the hotel, two keys splayed out in his hands like playing cards and a smile on his face. Affection spread through her body, pushing out her lingering irritation and relaxing her shoulders.

"I've got to go, Mom. I'll call you when I'm in Salt Lake. We can talk more then. If you're worried, you can talk to Babe. She met the guy." She hung up before her mom could continue to protest.

My guy. He wasn't, not really, but it was nice to think of Marc that way, only if for a moment.

"Your castle awaits, milady," Marc said as he climbed into the car. "The front desk staff said it was the nicest room in the place."

Selina looked over at the hotel. It was an older building, and she wasn't such a rural hick that she didn't realize it wasn't considered a "nice" hotel, but it still looked nicer than any hotel she had ever been in.

He brandished the hotel keys. "Nicest because it had the least road noise, that is. So we should get a good night's sleep. And two queen beds, as promised. I need to protect my virtue, after all," he said with a smile that was almost as floppy as his hair.

Her heart swelled at the same time that desire tingled between her legs. *Oh no.* The ache hinted that she was a lot closer to repeating the mistakes her mother had made than she wanted to be. At least her hunger had picked a good guy to direct its attentions at.

Their fingers brushed as she took one of the keys from him. Her body practically growled out how much it liked his touch. "Thank you," was all she had the ability to say.

He started the car back up, and they drove around to their parking spot in the back. They got their bags and walked up the stairs to their room with only enough conversation between them to coordinate roles.

Selina didn't know what to say. All the things she was feeling—affection, gratitude, yearning—whirled inside her, and all but the gratitude seemed inappropriate right now. She should say something, though. Especially as the lock clicked and he opened the door and there were two queen beds, as promised. He picked up both bags, setting hers on one bed and his on the other.

"Unless you want the one near the AC unit?" he asked with a nod to the metal box by the window. "I don't know which bed is the best bet for tonight."

She took a few tentative steps into the room. "Either is good for me."

"All right. Wake me up if you're freezing or too hot."

The next few steps she took were more certain. She was more certain. When she stopped in front of him, she took both his hands in hers. "Thank you."

He raised a brow. "For what?"

She stepped forward again, so they were closer but still holding hands. She could see the many different streaks of brown in his eyes. "For being you. For being the man I'd hoped you were while sitting across from you in a Chinese restaurant and wondering if I should say yes to your wild offer. For helping me feel safe and cared for, and for letting me have my space. There's so much more I could thank you for, but I don't have the words for any of it."

She stood on tiptoe. "So thank you," she said and pressed her lips against his cheek.

He leaned into her kiss, a small gasp of pleasure coming from his mouth as he tightened his hand around hers.

Their fingers remained intertwined as she pulled away from him, her heels connecting with the carpet again.

His eyes were a mix of confusion, longing, and anger. "I'm happy to have helped you, but I don't want kisses as a form of gratitude or payment or out of obligation. I thought we agreed on that."

"I kissed you because I wanted to," she said softly.

Desire flared in his eyes, pushing out the last heat of anger she'd seen in them. "Well, then," he said, pulling her forward.

She shuffled closer to him, her head tilting up at the same time his tilted down. Complications and unwanted implications of the kiss danced at the side of her vision, but she ignored them, sinking into his kiss as their lips connected. The last time she'd kissed a man had been forever ago. As Gary had gotten worse and worse, she'd avoided anything that smacked of a relationship.

But this was Marc, and every last part of her body screamed out that she could trust him. That they could share a kiss and nothing else. That he wouldn't hurt her. She could give herself this pleasure.

His lips were dry and a little rough from the winter air. Hers probably were, too, but any self-consciousness disappeared when he tilted his head and deepened the kiss. For a man who could be silly, his kisses were serious things. Dedication, study, and thought—all the things that he'd used to build a business that he could sell for millions of dollars before he was thirty were there in his kiss.

Their fingers were still intertwined when he moved his hands forward, pushing her hands back and behind her. He let go to grab on to her waist, pulling her even closer. The kiss had been good, the kiss had been nice, but this gentle but sure touch was what pushed her over the edge. The back of her throat tickled as she moaned.

She had to touch him. All of her had to touch him. Their lips weren't enough. And there was no way she was going to be the passive recipient of his caresses when she could reach out and run a hand through his hair. Stroke his neck. Run her fingers over his biceps and connect to his soul.

Or as close as she could come to his soul after having known him for a little over a day.

She held his jaw in her hands, desperate to keep him with her.

His grip on her body tightened, claiming her. She responded by moving her hands back to his hair and holding tight to him there. Her white knight. She'd never forget that he'd come into her life when she'd needed to be rescued, but she kissed him because his hair flopped about his face, he named his phones, and he was terrible at hitting on her. All those things about him made her heart swell with affection.

She let go, releasing her grip on his hair as if the strands were hot metal burning patterns into her skin. Part of him must have been expecting it because he dropped his hands from her waist immediately and stepped back.

They were both panting, chests rising and falling. His eyes looked as hooded and unfocused as hers felt. If she leaned in, she could kiss him again. He'd be open to it. He'd let her. And she'd enjoy it.

You're making my mistakes, echoed her mother's voice in her ears. Pregnant. Runaway. Stuck in Podunk, desperate to escape and too poor to attempt it. Trapped.

Marc wasn't Selina's father, though. At least she assumed they were very different people. She'd never met her father, but as far as she knew, her father hadn't had the dedication to make anything, much less a million-dollar app. And judging by how closely Marc was following the progress of his app, he didn't easily let go of things he created.

"Did I overstep my bounds?" he asked.

She shook her head, but it was a weak response. "No. No. I wanted that kiss as much as you did. But it's not a good idea. For so many reasons."

He nodded, slow and deliberate, as if he were still pushing away the desire webbing through his brain so he could think clearly. God knows she was still struggling to get her mind back to reality and *good decisions* and away from his kisses.

"You're right. You're absolutely right. I, uh, I've thought about kissing you since . . . well, since this morning when I woke up with you in my arms."

She raised a brow at him, and he laughed. "Okay, since before then. But throw me a bone. This moment, right now, wasn't the first time you'd thought about kissing me, either."

"No." She laughed now. He was easy to laugh around. "But we can't do it again."

"I agree. Absolutely."

"So it's settled, then? No kissing? This didn't change anything?"

He must have heard the question she hadn't asked because he took her hands in his again. "I said that I would take you to Salt Lake City and let you stay with me in my condo while you looked for a job. No matter what happens, I'll follow through on my promise." He squeezed her hand. "I swear to you, Selina. Do you believe me?"

She blinked away happy, reassured tears. "I believe you."

"Good. Let's go get some dinner. I asked the guy at the desk for a recommendation. He said the Flying J gas station had good food, as did the family diner. I suggest we try the diner."

With one last supportive squeeze of her hand, Marc stepped away from her. "Ready?"

The kiss and her conflicted feelings had her unsteady on her feet. She may not have kissed him because she was grateful, but desire still mixed with gratitude, which had her confused. Determined to hide the whirl of emotions swimming inside her, she put on her brightest smile, nodded, then grabbed her purse and followed him out the door.

Chapter Seven

$\mathcal{M}$ ARC'S PHONE BUZZED when he sat down in a booth at the diner. As soon as the waitress handed them their menus, he picked out a burger that seemed as if it would calm his hungry stomach fine, then pulled out his phone.

Another exec. Another fuck-off e-mail. At least this one was coming from someone higher up in the company this time. He was rating that high, at least. Even if they wouldn't let him have any say in his project.

"So what did you want to see tomorrow?" Selina's voice cracked through his focus on his phone.

"Hmm . . ." he said, scrolling through his list of e-mails from before the sale, looking for someone else to talk to about the project. *His* project.

"Tomorrow?" she prodded. "Come on. This is your fun vacation. I'm supposed to be along to help make it fun. And you said you wanted to see some sights. I think there are some caves nearby. We could visit those. And a waterfall. I don't know what else there is to see in southern Idaho."

"Those could all be interesting." He touched on an e-mail with *Session keys* in the subject line. That sounded promising. At least this guy was actually acknowledging Marc's idea. His attention locked on the lead, hunger for the work practically crawling up his skin until he could feel his fingers typing out the code.

God, he missed his work. He'd been so focused on selling Terry and being relieved that he didn't have to push himself into more sleepless nights that he'd never considered he might *miss* it. That he might want to be in the middle of everything. If he'd known, he would have followed Curtis and Terry to their new company.

"You've got one of your phones out. Do you want to look up those options? Maybe see what would be good before we get on the road so we have something to look forward to?"

"Listen, Selina." He didn't look up. "I appreciate what you're trying to do, but I'm busy with my project. I need to be left alone."

The loud intake of air he heard over the sound of "Winter Wonderland" did make him look up, though it didn't seem to be Selina who had made the insulted noise. The woman sitting across the table from him had eyes wide with shock and was sitting back in her booth as if he'd slapped her.

He looked to his left. The waitress must have made that noise because she reached out and yanked their menus away, nearly spilling his water in the process.

"What can I get you?" the waitress asked Selina, all kindness and consideration. She didn't have the same tone of voice for Marc, and he hoped his fries didn't come back burned.

"That was rude," Selina said after the waitress had walked off.

"I'm sorry." Hell, even he could hear that he didn't sound all that sorry. "Really, I am. I just think I can finally get someone to listen to me and let me work on the project again."

"Why is it so important to you?" She pulled her glass of water toward her and wrapped her lips around the straw. Her sexy lips, the ones that felt amazing when they'd kissed his, the ones he wanted to kiss again.

He shook the image out of his head. "Terry is *my* project. Oh, it's Curtis's, too, but it was my idea. And now I have an idea that would make it even better. Make it cleaner. When the app is fully launched, I want it to be the best it can be. Even with the company's name on the app, enough people in the industry will know it's my work, and I can't let it get out into the wild without it being anything less than perfect."

It wasn't only his reputation at stake, though. He wanted the work.

The straw slid out of her mouth, leaving a ring of red lipstick behind. "But you've talked to Curtis about it, right? Maybe he's already working on it."

"If he is, he hasn't told me." And it was Marc's idea. *He* wanted to work on it.

Even in his head, he could hear that he sounded like a child denied a favorite toy. Maybe he was being possessive and should let go of Terry, but would it kill Curtis to respond?

She shrugged. "But you sold it to the biggest technology company in the world. They have an entire campus of people dedicated to stuff like this. I read online that their meter maids are robots. They'll figure your idea out, especially if you've shared the basics. And your friend took a job there, right? So he knows the project as well as you do. It sounds like they have all the reasons in the world to implement your idea, and you can go on enjoying your vacation."

Yeah, but that didn't mean his friend should give him the cold shoulder. He should at least give him the courtesy of a real e-mail. None of this brush-off shit.

What Selina was saying made sense, but it didn't change the basic facts of the situation. This was *his* project and *he* wanted to fix it.

"You don't understand," he said.

The waitress set plates of food in front of them. Suspiciously, Marc picked up the bun on his burger and looked at his dinner. Everything seemed fine, and the fries looked perfectly cooked. He picked a couple up and shoved them in his mouth, the hot, salty oil dripping down his throat, coating and softening some of his irritation.

Man, he was hungry. He should make sure to buy more snacks for the drive tomorrow.

"You're right," Selina said, her sharp tone catching his attention and popping his head up. She hadn't touched her food yet, and her arms were crossed over her chest. "I don't understand. But what I don't understand is why you haven't tossed your phones out of the window so you can enjoy your vacation. Do you know how many people would love to be in your shoes right now? Money in the bank. Bills paid off. No boss to report to. An empty road and a good time ahead of you."

"Well, I'm not totally the man of leisure with no commitments. I've got you to worry about. God, and maybe I'm worried too much about my job that was, but you've got no plan. Nothing. That's why you're here."

This time it *was* Selina who sucked in a breath. He shouldn't have implied she was a burden and a commitment, especially since he wanted her on this trip.

No. He *needed* her on this trip.

He closed his eyes and rubbed his forehead with his fingertips, but the words didn't magically work their way back into his mouth and down his throat. Taking back words as cutting as that wasn't as easy as deleting bad code, and its effects could be just as malicious.

"I'm sorry," he said, desperate to stem the damage he'd done. "I didn't mean that."

"Didn't you?"

God, the way her voice sank inside her, almost turning her inside out, nearly broke his heart. It had seemed like the farther away from her hometown they'd gotten, the bigger Selina had gotten, like suddenly she was willing to throw a couple of elbows if she needed to get people out of her way. And in a split second, he'd managed to shrink her back inside herself.

He felt like a heel. A heel with dog shit on it. And cat shit, for good measure.

Her shrug was barely noticeable. "You're paying for my dinner, and you paid for the hotel room, but I hope you don't think you have to *take care of me.*" She said the last words with a shudder, and he didn't blame her for it.

"I thought we were two people helping each other out," she went on. "Me keeping you company and you making it so that I have enough money for a security deposit on a place when we get to Salt Lake. Wasn't that the deal??" Her brows were raised, matching the new higher octave of her voice. "Maybe looking for a job and seeing about community college doesn't seem like a plan to you, but it is to me."

"It is a plan," he offered. "And I'm not angry at you." He reached his arms out across the table, palms up, but she didn't offer hers in return.

He kept them there, his fingers jutting up into the sky, lost and alone without her fingers intertwined in his. "What I said before, about you being a better story of hard work and courage than me was true. I meant every word."

She gave that fucking nearly invisible shrug again. The one he wished she would replace with words, even if it meant she'd be yelling at him. "I guess."

His belief that he was mature enough not to blurt out stupid shit was clearly wrong. He'd hurt Selina. That was worse than Curtis and company not responding to his e-mails. He needed a couple of beers so he could forget how annoyed he was with everyone for not following his sensible plans, and how annoyed he was with himself for letting them get to him enough that he took it out on Selina.

Or maybe more than a six-pack, he needed a walk. To stretch his legs and his mind and stop being cooped up in the car. He'd feel better once he got to the resort. Until then, though, he'd need to apologize to Selina more sincerely. When he'd calmed down, that was.

The waitress refilled his water and he and Selina finished their dinner in a chilly silence that he couldn't wait to get out of. At least once they were in their hotel room, he could turn on the television and drown out the boom of her hurt and the echo of the words that he'd said to her, which was now running through his mind on repeat.

When he wasn't trying to think of what to write to convince Curtis—or anyone—to listen to him.

After paying the bill, he practically ran to the car to get away from the funk he had left behind in the seats. He was in the car and had the motor running before Selina was even halfway across the parking lot. His tires squealed as he shifted into reverse and backed up.

It wasn't until he'd pulled up next to her and realized she was standing perfectly still, her purse clutched against her chest, that it occurred to him it looked as if he was about to drive away on her and leave her there in the middle of nowhere.

The fact that he was acting like every other loser guy in her life startled him. Waiting until he'd cooled down wouldn't cut it for Selina. He wasn't being the kind of person he wanted to be for her.

He rolled down the window. "I'm sorry for being a dick. There's no excuse for it."

Still clearly shaken, she nodded and got in.

On the short drive through the town's two stoplights, Marc took several deep breaths. He hadn't meant what he'd said to Selina, but he didn't know how to make her believe him. He liked his life organized and well planned, and he didn't understand how she wasn't freaked out by the sudden and massive turn her life just took. He'd gotten the change in his life that he'd worked years for, and still, here he was, obsessively checking his e-mail, trying to get the life he'd once had back. Maybe he couldn't give up his project, but that wasn't Selina's fault.

When they hit a grocery store, he pulled into the lot and turned the car off. After the radio stopped, Selina's silence pulsed through the inside of the car.

"I'm sorry," he said.

"Yes, you said. Apology accepted." She was saying the right words, but the lack of warmth in her tone smarted. Though her tone surely cut less than what he'd said to her. Besides, he wasn't looking to win this argument or shake her until she understood how sorry he was. He wanted her to feel better because he liked her. Because he respected her. Because he really was sorry. And because what it was like being in her shoes was beyond anything he could imagine.

"Yes, I already said it, but I don't think I said it well enough. I didn't mean what I said, Selina. I promise. I lost control of my baby—I *sold* control of my baby—and this trip hasn't helped me come to terms with that fact. But—" He stopped himself before he launched into more about his own frustrations. "But that's not what's important right now. It doesn't matter why I said what I said. It doesn't change the fact that I hurt you. And I'm sorry for that."

Her entire body seemed to relax at once. He'd said the magic words, and even better, they were true. He'd meant every one of them.

"Thank you," she said, turning her head to give him a slight smile. "I appreciate and accept your apology. It's hard for me to understand how your life is causing you stress right now, but just because I don't understand it doesn't mean it's not happening. And I know that stress can make even the best people say things they don't mean." She paused a beat. "And I think you're one of the best people."

They didn't say much to each other on the drive back to the hotel, but at least there was no silence pushing down on the car.

Back in their room, he turned on the television for background noise while he applied for a job at the company that bought Terry—maybe it was a way to get back in. But he didn't need the television for company. Selina, sitting on her bed flipping through her phone, provided that and more.

Chapter Eight

THE BUZZ OF the heater might as well have been a mosquito buzzing directly in Selina's ears for all she was able to relax her mind and sleep. The highway noise couldn't drown it out, though she was at least honest enough with herself to admit that the cars would be keeping her awake if the blowing air wasn't already doing it.

She rolled over in bed, kicking at her sheet. *No plan.* Marc's words knocked on her subconscious every time she got anywhere remotely near sleep. The problem wasn't that he'd said the words—though they had hurt like a large, sharp needle. The problem was that they were true. Taking one class per semester at a community college and working at a diner until she could escape wasn't a plan. It had been an existence, and she'd been lucky that Marc had been the one to walk into Babe's Diner and give her this opportunity.

She sighed. That had been more of a plan than what she currently had, which was find a job and a place to live. But how? God, how would she do it in the week she had the use of Marc's hotel room at the ski resort? She'd e-mailed her professor, both about her final assignment and the gallery, but that wasn't really a plan, either. That was a shot in the dark.

She pushed the sheets down and sat up. She didn't want to rely on Marc. They were both lost and wandering. If she asked—or even looked like she might need it—he would probably be willing to find a place in Salt Lake City—pestering his friend through texts and e-mail—and she could be adrift again, just in a bigger city. The jokes they had shared and the intimate conversations would become sore as they became the only thing holding each other up.

Resolved to make a plan past the week at the resort, she swung her legs over the side of the bed, grabbed her phone, and tiptoed her way to the bathroom. Door shut and light on, Selina posted to Facebook that she needed a job and a room in Salt Lake City, starting immediately. Most of the people she knew from high school had gone to Spokane when they'd left for the "big city," but a few had ended up in Salt Lake, and if they didn't have any leads, maybe they knew someone who did. She texted Babe, too. Maybe Babe's friend knew of something or someone that could help.

Her business done, she flipped the light off and snuck back out of the bathroom. Enough light streamed through the window that she could make out Marc's sleeping form. He was sleeping in a T-shirt and his boxers, a far cry from last night when they'd both been sleeping in as many layers as they'd been able to put on.

He was handsome and kind, and as soon as she found a place to live, she'd never see him again. The realization made her sad . . . and lonely. It would be nice to have someone she was more than Facebook acquaintances with in Salt Lake. More importantly, it would have been nice to continue to know Marc. Maybe they could exchange e-mails after he returned to Seattle after his adventures. Or wherever it was he was going to go next.

Or maybe when he dropped her off at wherever she was going to be, that would be the end of this. If she wanted anything more to happen with him than that kiss she could still feel on her lips, she would need to act now.

Before she'd realized what she was even considering, she was sitting on the edge of his bed and had placed her hand on his shoulder.

Marc stirred, then murmured a soft, "Hmm?"

"I couldn't sleep. Can I get in bed with you?"

"Hmm?" he muttered again. "Oh . . . yes, uh, of course." He scooted over, taking most of the sheets and blankets with him. But then he shifted around, reaching around behind him and lifting the covers and sheets off himself. He gave them a good yank so that she had covers now, too, as well as space in the bed and someone to cuddle with.

When she got in bed, she rolled over to her side, and he curled up around her like they had been navigating sharing a bed for years. His hand rested on her stomach as they spooned. The light touch stirred desire deep in her belly, want tingling between her legs.

And curiosity.

She knew how Marc's lips felt under hers, but how would his chest feel as she rubbed her hands against it? And how would he feel when poised above her, about to enter her?

She rolled over so that they were facing each other. He woke enough to shift so that their legs were intertwined. He was semihard against her leg.

Does he have a condom? The thought flitted through her mind before she leaned forward and kissed him.

He responded immediately, pressing his lips against hers and weaving his hands around her head and threading them through her hair, holding her tightly against him. She rocked closer to him. Feeling him hard against her leg wasn't enough. Feeling his hands in her hair and his lips on hers wasn't enough. She wanted more.

She shoved her hands under the waistband of his boxers, digging her fingernails into his perfect butt and pulling him closer to her.

In an instant, he had flipped her onto her back and climbed on top of her, fitting himself between her legs. His hard length, covered by the thin cotton of his boxers, was pressed against her. "Oh, Selina, you feel so good," he groaned as he rocked against her.

She yanked up his shirt, tugging at it trying to get it off. His arms got caught in the sleeves as they both struggled for a moment to pull it over his head. While he was still propped up on his arms, she skimmed her palms over his now-bare chest. His soft chest hair tickled. He sighed, relaxing into her. Then, with a low growl of frustration and desire, he pulled at her shirt, and they had another moment of struggle to get her T-shirt off. This time, they bumped heads and giggled.

"Do you have a condom?" she whispered as soon as his hands hit the elastic of her pajama shorts.

"Hmm?" he murmured, nibbling at her neck. "Oh! Yes. Don't move."

"What if I move to take off my shorts?" she asked with a wiggle of her hips.

He smiled, then kissed her neck, her ears, and finally her lips. "I suppose that's okay," he teased.

He lifted off her and swung off the bed. As he stood by the side of the bed, she admired the shape of his body, the dark shadows of him backlit by streetlights.

From this moment on, she would recognize his body anywhere. The smell and feel of him was etched in her memory. Her *body* would recognize him. She could feel him in her skin, in her muscles, and in her bones. In her marrow.

She heard his suitcase unzip. He rustled through clothes and then unzipped another pocket. As he returned, he was ripping at the foil packet. Her hips pushed forward and up, wanting him. She was impatient by the time he was standing next to the bed. Their hands intertwined and their bodies writhed and bumped as he tried to put the condom on while she tried to pull off his boxers. Desire deepened the sounds of his chuckles, and her giggles sped into moans.

Suddenly his shorts were off and the condom was on. He was on top of and then inside her. They both sighed, shifting and undulating until he was deep inside her.

She couldn't touch as much of him as she needed, but she tried. Kisses met shoulders and arms and necks and ears and cheeks. Hands explored backs and butts and rubbed against chests, fingers digging in to skin as their breathing grew more labored and faster until they both cried out at once.

Selina lifted up her hips as Marc bucked several times, groaning with satisfaction until he nearly collapsed on top of her, his arms stopping his fall only once he was a breath away from her.

"Hi," she said, suddenly a bit shy and weary from the force of her orgasm.

"Hi." His kiss on her jaw shook the shy feeling away, and she kissed him back.

"I'll be right back," he said as he climbed off her.

His shadow retreated into the bedroom. The faucet turned on, then off, and then he was climbing back into bed with her, wrapping his arms around her and pulling her toward him as if they had been doing this for years.

And as if they had years to keep doing this.

She pushed that thought to the back of her mind, willing herself to focus on the pleasantness of the present as she drifted off to sleep.

MARC LAY IN bed, feeling just about perfect. He was warm, satiated, and Selina's body fit perfectly against his, even if his right arm was beginning to fall asleep. He smiled as the perfect solution to his restlessness sprang into his head. Selina could come with him for the rest of his winter trip. His mind swayed off to sleep, buoyed by his dreams of the future and Selina.

Chapter Nine

SELINA CLUTCHED THE handhold above the passenger window as they bounced over the snow-dusted, rutted dirt road to the ice caves. As with the bird sanctuary the day before, this area of Idaho lacked heavy snow and high winds blew what little snow there was up in swirls. Swaths of black lava studded the landscape, a break between the dead grass and tops of sagebrush. Finally, they sprang their way under an arch announcing the ice caves and pulled into the parking lot.

There were three buildings, all made of logs and one clearly a house, probably for the people who ran the caves. One of the buildings was small, with restroom signs nailed to the wood. The largest building also had a sign for the caves—this one smaller and over the door. Between all the buildings and off to the side of the parking lot were statues, the smallest one taller than the roof of the buildings and the tallest one towering over the parking lot. There were several Native Americans, a couple of cavemen and cavewomen, and one dinosaur.

Marc put the SUV in park and turned the car off. "Well, should we go in and see what they've got?" he asked. "Though the statues alone might be worth the drive."

His voice was warm and loving. It had been since they'd woken up this morning, naked limbs tangled together and a satisfied, safe feeling deep in her bones.

"You wanted to see the odd roadside attractions in Idaho, didn't you?" She nodded her head to the statutes. "Those look about as odd as they come."

"I don't understand the dinosaur."

She laughed. "Neither do I."

"Come on," he said, patting her knee. "Let's see what this is all about."

They both hopped out of the car and trotted to the information building. They didn't hold hands, though they stood close enough that their hands brushed each other as they walked. When they reached the door, Marc gave it a hard tug. It was locked.

"Hey," a voice called out from the porch. "We're closed for the winter."

They both turned around. An old man, with deep wrinkles and enough sun damage that Selina couldn't tell his age beyond *old*, trundled toward them. A worn cowboy hat was pulled low over his head, and the work boots on his feet had clearly seen better days.

"Your website said to call for winter hours," Marc said.

"Well, did you call?"

"Yeah," Marc confirmed. "And no one answered."

The man had crossed the parking lot and was now

standing right in front of them. "If you called the number on the website, that one's old. The missus and I don't know how to change it, and our son keeps saying he'll do it later."

"How long has it been like that?"

"Couple years," the man said with a shrug. "Most people out this way are more interested in skiing than in caves, so we don't get many visitors, especially in the winter."

"Can we have a tour anyway?" Marc asked.

"Caves are closed up for the season. Ain't much to see."

"I'll update your website for you," Marc offered.

Selina watched with interest as both Marc and the old man seemed to settle into faces primed for negotiation. The old man looked Marc up and down, glanced as his new SUV, and finally said, "That's not enough to open the caves."

"And we'll pay you the tour cost."

The old man considered them both, his keen eye noting Marc's expensive ski jacket and Selina's worn winter coat. "Where are you both from?"

"I'm from Athol," Selina said, at the same time Marc said, "Seattle."

"Which one is it?"

"I'm from Athol," she answered. "Marc is from Seattle. He's giving me a ride to Salt Lake City, and we're stopping at touristy spots along the way."

"That so." The man rubbed at the white stubble on

his chin. "That all seems a far bit out of your way. How do I know you can fix the website?"

"If you have the password, I can fix it."

"He's real smart with computers," Selina attested, then giggled at the understatement.

"It's on the fridge, for all that I know what to do with it."

"Not only will I update your website but I'll teach you how to do it yourself."

The old man nodded once. "Son, you have yourself a tour."

They were welcomed into the house and greeted by an older woman, also of indeterminate age, who smiled at the idea of their website being fixed and bustled off to get them some coffee. The furniture in the house was sparse, and what was there was threadbare. But after their coats had been hung up, they were led to a fairly new computer.

"Nice," Marc said with a nod at the flat screen monitor and desktop CPU, whose red power buttons glowed. "This will be even easier. I was afraid I was going to have to engineer something fancy because of ancient web browsers. But we should get this done in no time."

"I'll get the password for you, then," the old man said.

He returned with a piece of paper, and his wife followed, clutching four mugs of coffee in her hands. The mugs were blue metal with white splotches. *Campware,* Selina recognized.

"Before I get started, I'm Marc." He tilted his head toward Selina. "And this is Selina. Thanks for agreeing to the tour."

"I'm Jeremiah," the man said. "And this here's Phyllis."

"Jeremiah and Phyllis," Selina said. "It's a pleasure to meet you." She accepted her cup of coffee from Phyllis, then they both turned to watch Marc and Jeremiah at the computer.

"How long have you lived here?" Selina asked Phyllis.

"Oh, since I married Jeremiah. He's my second husband. He was born here, and the ice caves have been in his family since they came west. All the good farmin' land's been sold. We make what little money we can off tours and such. There's a gift shop in the big building."

"You don't give the tours, do you?" Selina was horrified at the idea of this old couple taking several tours a day into caves.

"Not anymore, no. We get a couple of our grandkids down every summer. They know all the good stories, and they give the tours. They need the tip money. We run the gift shop." Phyllis shrugged and took a sip of her coffee. "Not sure who's going to take the place over once we leave. None of the grandkids want it—our son sure don't—and I don't know that I'd want them to have it. Good enough life for Jeremiah and me, but not much of a life for anyone else, I suppose."

Now that Selina's coffee had cooled down a little, she

took a sip of the strong, bracing brew. If this was what they drank every day, it was no wonder they were spry enough to run a gift shop and tourist attraction.

The two women continued to make small talk while Marc walked Jeremiah through all the steps of logging in to their website—which Marc had been excited to learn was a Wordpress site—and how to change content. He had the older man sign in and sign back out of the site several times until both men were confident he could do it on his own. Then Marc asked Phyllis to sit down and repeat the process.

When they'd finished, Marc dug into his pocket and pulled out his wallet. He gave what appeared to be business cards to the couple, one each. "These are my personal cards. I can help you with almost anything you need on the computer, and I can probably teach you how to do it over the phone."

"That's mighty kind of you." The old man looked at his wife. "I'll be honest . . . I wasn't real sure you'd be able to help us. Strangers, you know."

"If you like," Phyllis interrupted, "I'll make you lunch while Jeremiah gives you the tour. Least we can do to thank you."

Marc caught Selina's eye over the couple's head, and she nodded. "That sounds great, Phyllis. I've been eating out for a week and would appreciate a home-cooked meal."

Jeremiah handed them their coats. "Let's go, then."

Back to being bundled up, Marc and Selina followed

the old man out of the house. He led them on a trail through bits of lava rock and sagebrush, past more statues—smaller ones, this time—and to a dugout in the rocks where there was a small door.

As they walked, Marc held Selina's hand while he chatted with the old man. Jeremiah told them stories too far-fetched to be believed, though they were fun to hear. They included train robbers and a missing trunk of gold, a Shoshone girl who had escaped her capture from another Native American tribe and had hidden out among the caves, and at least one Wild West shoot-out. Though, by the huge grin on Jeremiah's face, she could tell the shoot-out was one he'd made up just for them.

Through the door, he led them along a wooden path that had been built over a slick of ice. Stalactites hung down from the ceiling, and stalagmites busted up out of the ice.

"This is really cool," Marc said, leaning over to whisper in her ear.

His warm breath—and mouth simply being so close to her neck—sent shivers down her spine. "Yeah. I'm glad we could come here."

"Hard to tell that the caves are cold when it's cold outside," Jeremiah said, continuing his tour, "but they're thirty degrees in the summer, too. My parents used to store their meat down here before electricity and before they started tourin'."

He went on to tell them about the natural history of the caves, the geology of the local area, and a little bit about some of the other caves off the highway. "But this is the only one with ice," he said proudly.

Selina couldn't help but smile. Not only at Jeremiah, but at the fact that not once during their entire tour did Marc let go of her hand.

Maybe, she thought as they shared lunch and conversation in Phyllis and Jeremiah's small kitchen, if the gallery job turned out to be a dead end and Babe's friend couldn't help her, she'd see if Marc wanted company on the rest of his winter vacation. The past two days had been the most fun she could ever remember having. And while the birds of prey sanctuary was neat and the ice caves were cool, it wasn't the sights that had made the past couple of days so wonderful. It had been Marc.

Seeing him with Phyllis and Jeremiah only made her like him more. He'd been kind and understanding as he'd talked them through their website and had genuinely seemed interested in their lives. The older couple, too, seemed to see the same warmth and trustworthiness in him that had convinced her to get in the SUV and drive away with him in the first place. He was a solid, hardworking man, which was exactly what she wanted in her life.

Or she was sure he could be, if he stopped his wanderings. She hoped she was smart enough not to expect him to be something he wasn't—or something he didn't want to be.

After lunch and good-byes, her phone buzzed as she was climbing into the car. She pulled it out of her pocket and checked her messages. The ones she had been hoping for last night were there, but her heart fell as she read them. Babe's friend had a room she could rent, and her professor thought he might be able to help her get a job at the gallery. Everything she'd hoped for in Salt Lake City was coming together, just as she was thinking of throwing it all away and becoming as free as Marc.

Only she'd never be free like Marc. She didn't have the money for it.

"Have you ever thought about staying in Salt Lake?" she asked as they turned onto the main highway.

"What? No." He shook his head as if to emphasize his point. "I've had this idea of a trip planned ever since Curtis and I decided to sell Terry. I'm not giving it up."

She looked back at her phone, disappointment sinking her heart like the *Titanic*.

"Looking forward to the falls?" he asked, his voice chipper, insensitive to her hurt. But of course he wouldn't know. He was still operating under the rules of their original agreement.

"Yeah," she said, determined to spend the drive from the ice caves to the waterfall reminding herself of her dream and how close she was to it, Marc or no Marc.

Chapter Ten

"ARE YOU SURE you know how to get to the falls?" Selina asked, her voice as doubtful as her expression as she gazed out the windows at the sagebrush dotting the side of the road.

"These are the directions I found online. And my GPS is sending me to the same place, so this must be it." But he really wasn't very sure of it, either. There wasn't much out here besides the sagebrush and large houses spaced almost a quarter mile apart.

"Have a little confidence in technology," he said. "After all, technology failures led me to you, so even if it's wrong, it'll be right." At the memory, he broke into a wide smile. "Besides, we went over that massive canyon about ten minutes ago. The falls have to be around here somewhere."

They started to descend into the canyon. Then they passed a closed pay station for the parking lot. They were in the right place. The town's website had said there was only a fee during the summer. They had their pick of parking spaces and there wasn't anyone else with them as they walked out to the viewing area.

"Huh," Selina said. "I've heard of Shoshone Falls, of course, but I'm not sure what I expected."

Massive gray stones stepped down from the river before morphing into a cliff that plunged over two hundred feet. Water streamed over the cliffs, not in one big sheet, but in several smaller waterfalls spanning the breadth of the canyon. On the far side of the river was a red-roofed white building that was probably several stories tall but was dwarfed by the magnitude of the cliffs.

The view was pretty, no question about that. But it wasn't the massive flow of water they had both expected. Less disappointing than not seeing wolves with the Wolf People and a closed submarine museum in the middle of northern Idaho, but still ... At least Selina was with him.

Marc pulled out his favorite phone. The website for the falls was still up and he skimmed the information again. "Ah. The falls are best viewed in the late spring and early summer when the snow runoff is at its highest. We should come back."

She made a noncommittal noise. Her face was as unreadable. Still, it wasn't a no, and this was probably the best opportunity Marc would have to broach his idea.

"I've had a great time today," he said. "And yesterday, with you at the bird sanctuary." He gathered up all his excitement, then took a deep breath so that he didn't bowl her over with his enthusiasm. "After Snowdance,

I've got hotel rooms booked all around the Rocky Mountains, with a week in between each place for driving around and seeing the sights. You should come with me. I'll bring you back to Salt Lake. Or Denver. Or Tahoe. Or whatever city you want to be in when we're done. Come have fun with me."

She blinked, and his heart sank.

"I've got plans," she said.

"Since when?" Being lost felt like a waste of time and the e-mails he was getting back about his project were disheartening, but it was all okay with Selina next to him. The idea of her not being there was suddenly unbearable.

"Since we left the caves. Babe's friend can rent me a room in Salt Lake. It's near some bus lines so I can get to work once I find something, and it's not far from the community college campus. It's not much, but it's everything I need right now. And my professor thought me working in the gallery was possible. His friend needs someone on a part-time basis. With a waitressing job, I could make it work. Maybe even to save up a little money. Get my independence back."

The word *independence* registered in his mind but not before his heart fell out of his body and landed at his feet with as much force as he imagined went over the falls in front of them at peak season.

His mind climbed around and over that word, trying to figure out why she would choose to live in a *rented* room, ride the bus, and work two jobs when she could be driving around the west with him, skiing at some of the best resorts in the world. "I'll pay for your ski lessons," he offered. "It'll be fun."

She leaned forward to rest her arms on the railing, then looked over her shoulder at him. "It's not the ski lessons or the hotels or the meals. Or the fun. I don't think you're having fun."

"I'm having fun with you." He folded his arms on the railing, too, their skin barely touching. He needed to touch her, to know she was still next to him, at least for this moment.

"I guess." She shook her head, her blond hair bouncing around her face. The hair that had caught his attention only a couple of days ago. The hair he might never see again.

"No," she corrected herself. "I see that you are. But you've never stopped checking your phones, and it's not like you're not scrolling Facebook. You're waiting for an e-mail saying you can be let back in to the project that you sold. And if that e-mail comes through, well, I'm sure you'll do as you promised and get me to whatever city I want to be in, but you'll drop this man-of-leisure act in a heartbeat and every minute more you have to spend fulfilling your promise to me will be time you resent."

"That's not . . ." He was going to say it wasn't true, but it was. And he wasn't a liar. "I won't get an e-mail inviting me to work on the project." His heart was already on the ground and admitting the truth felt like his heart was now being kicked over the rocks. By feet shod in cleats. "I applied for a job at the company that bought Terry. Curtis sent my application back to me with an e-mail that said, *You're making a fool of yourself.*" He clenched his fists in frustration. "I don't know what else to do besides keep driving around and skiing. I'm done with the project of my life."

He felt hollow and full of holes. Anything that got poured into him was going to drain right out. A sieve. A waste.

"Your choices aren't just *get back on the project* or *be a man of leisure.*" Her brows were crossed in confusion, wrinkles covering her forehead. "You can do something else."

"Something else like you're doing? Finding a wait-ressing job and going back to community college?" His anger burned through the holes littering his body as he said the words, and it didn't feel good. Nothing about this conversation felt good.

It all felt *wrong.* As if he was being dumped when they weren't even dating. Only it wasn't like the other times he'd been dumped. Once, in college, he'd felt like a child being denied a toy. And then when he was working on his project, a woman had dumped him because she never saw him. She must have been right, too, because he didn't remember missing her.

But Marc wanted to have fun with Selina. He wanted to explore with her and get to know her better, see those moments when she was relaxed and when her face puckered into the strangely hot irritation that made her lips purse.

They weren't a couple, and all she was asking for was their original agreement, but he still felt as though he was being rejected because he was at odds with himself. As though there were some defect in him that made him unworthy.

It's not because you're lost. It's because you're not trying to find yourself.

All the code running through his mind suddenly finished processing and his brain flashed with a result. She'd said something about him that was both true and something he didn't like, and he'd responded by throwing accusations at her.

Not a way to plead his case.

He was silent for moment, letting the noise of the falls wash over him and the icy winter water cool the ashes his anger had left behind.

"Maybe my plans don't look like much to you," she said. "Maybe it looks like I'm just replacing my Idaho life with a Utah one. But my goal was to get away from my stepfather and my small town, and I did that. I might even have a chance to live my own dream and work in a gallery, something I never could have done in Athol. And I won't be dependent on you for everything I eat and every bed I sleep on. That's as important as my dreams."

Without his anger at himself now roaring through his ears, reason managed to sneak in. She had a dream and she had the chance to pursue it. Even if he could get in the way of that, he wouldn't want to. One dream of his own life was done; he needed to find a new one. And she was right. He wasn't even *trying* to find something. He'd given himself the winter of every skier's fantasy, and he was going to blow it because he'd decided he couldn't be happy without Terry to work on.

He had to at least try for something more. He had to make use of his winter hiatus to step away from Terry and see what he wanted to do next, figure out who he was without Terry to work on or Curtis to work with. And he couldn't hang around Selina, using her as a crutch to distract him from the fact that he was treading water just as much as she had been.

That realization hurt, though not nearly as much as the knowledge that he might not see Selina again. That realization *burned*.

She turned her face away from him to the waterfalls. Shoshone Falls in winter wasn't the massive Niagara-like sight he'd been led to believe, but the water cascading over the rocks soothed the rough edges of his soul. The sight was no less beautiful for being different from what he'd expected.

"When we get to Salt Lake and you drop me off at the house with my room, I'll have reached one of my goals, and I'm on my way to creating new ones. Bigger ones," she went on. "So maybe achieving just one goal doesn't look like much to you, but at least I'm not stopping there."

He nodded slowly. "I get it. It took me awhile, but I

get it. And I get that you're making progress and I'm not. And that I'm relying on you to distract me." Sadness pulled at him, a sinking feeling that seemed to drag at his muscles and bones. "I guess I need to figure myself out on my own . . . So let's get you to Salt Lake."

He put his hand on her back, thinking they would return to the parking lot. Instead, she leaned into him for a hug, resting her head on his shoulder. He laid his head on the top of hers, the smell of hotel shampoo filling his nose. He'd have to avoid staying at that same chain of hotels for the rest of his winter trip because he wouldn't be able to resist opening the shampoo just so he could smell this moment, remembering her in his arms.

She sniffed a couple of times, and he realized that she was crying. When he was younger, it might have bothered him. Emotions had been scary and code had been clean. But now he understood her strength and admired the way she pushed through her troubles to carve out a life for herself. If crying was a part of that, then he admired that, too.

He didn't know how long they stood there, but when she finally pulled away, he knew it hadn't been long enough. She had come into his life like a feather, blown in by the wind, when he needed her strength and she needed his freedom. And she was leaving just as softly.

They walked to the car in silence. In fact, they drove the four hours to Salt Lake City mostly in silence. What was there left to say?

Chapter Eleven

THE WINTER SUN was setting as Marc drove them down a series of narrow residential streets lined with bungalows. Selina peered out the window at her new neighborhood—at least for the foreseeable future—trying to read the people who lived in the houses.

In early December, much of the greenery was dead, but there wasn't any snow to cover up the brown plants and dry grass. There was smog, though. She hadn't realized that Salt Lake City had so much smog. The gray haze wasn't the crisp mountain air that she had expected.

"The neighborhood looks nice," Marc said, sounding relieved.

The last leg of their trip had been four hours of un-comfortable silence, with only minimal talking when they stopped for gas and a snack. Selina hadn't known what to say, and she suspected Marc hadn't, either. Now he sounded both reassured and grateful for something to talk about.

Multicolored Christmas lights covered the railings of the porch of the next house, and the light by the front door was on. She looked at the number on the mailbox and took a deep breath. They were really here.

When they pulled to a stop at the curb, the front door opened. A woman of Babe's age, nearly as thin as Babe was large, walked out. "Selina?" she asked, walking toward them.

Backlit by the setting sun, the woman was hard to see, but her voice sounded kind. Of course, Selina would trust Babe with anything, so any friend of Babe's had to be good people.

"Yes," Selina said as she climbed out of the car. "It's me. And you're Pam?"

To her surprise, Pam rushed up and enveloped her in a hug. "It's nice to meet you, my dear. Babe and I are old friends, back from when her first husband was in the Army. She's always spoken so highly of you."

"It's nice to meet you, too." Selina turned to look at Marc, who had walked up to them. "And this is Marc. He gave me a ride down here." That seemed like such an understatement for what he meant to her. "And a friend."

Still an understatement, but a better one. He was her rescuer, but now with her own room to rent—arranged by her—she was going to be her own rescuer. The thought gave her strength and hope for the future.

"Nice to meet you, Marc," Pam said, shaking his hand. "Why don't you get Selina's bag and come in to the house? You can set it in her room."

Marc and Selina dutifully followed Pam into the house and to Selina's new bedroom.

"This is nice," Marc said, and Selina realized that he'd been more worried about her than she had been. That realization was made sweeter because he wasn't trying to stop her and he hadn't used his worry or dire threats to try and convince her to stay with him.

Like the rest of the house, the room was very clean, if simply decorated, and filled with old, worn furniture. It was clear Pam took pride in her house, though she didn't seem to have much money to spend on it.

"I'm so glad you had a room to rent," Selina said.

"Honey, you're helping me out as much as I'm helping you. I don't know if Babe told you, but I'm still paying off medical bills from cancer two years ago. This income will be very helpful. And the food-and-utilities split works for you?"

Selina nodded.

"Good." Pam put her hands on her hips and gave a curt but not unfriendly nod. Like Babe, Pam seemed to be a woman who didn't let warmth and love get in the way of practicality. "I've got a lease printed out over on the dining table. Can't be too careful with these things, even if you are a friend of Babe's."

"That seems smart," Selina said.

As Selina followed Pam out of the bedroom, Marc put his hand on the small of her back. The simple gesture of support meant more to her than she could ever express in words. He stood by her as she read over and signed the lease.

"I've got dinner on the stove. Selina, you're welcome

to have some. Marc, do you want to stay for dinner?"

Selina tried not to hope for another hour with Marc, but that was as impossible as not needing to breathe.

"No, thank you. I called Snowdance and arranged a room for tonight. I'd like to drive up the mountain before it gets too dark."

"I'll walk you out," Selina said quickly. She didn't want him to leave without having a chance for them to talk privately. They didn't need an audience for the end of this relationship.

Out in the cold, standing by Marc's SUV, Selina shivered.

"Feel okay about this situation?" he asked.

"Yes. It will be good." She wasn't simply saying that; she actually believed it. Pam was kind. She'd seen the bus lines down the street. There were almost always waitressing jobs available, and then there was a matter of college, of course, but that could wait a couple of months. She might get a job at a gallery, and if not, she could volunteer at one of the art museums. Babe was already working on selling her car, too, so the money from that would give Selina a little safety net.

"More than good," she said, her voice stronger in the crisp night air. "I'm in a much better place right now, and I have you to thank for it. I'm not sure I'll ever be able to repay you."

Being here, she realized that it hadn't even been the money that had been keeping her in her hometown. She had needed a push. And a pull. Gary had provided one;

Marc had provided the other.

Only, it wasn't just gratitude that was welling up in her chest. Marc was the man she had needed at the time, but in another life, in another situation, she would have liked to develop their relationship more. The affection warming her down to the tips of her toes could turn into love if she let it.

He put his hands on her shoulders, rubbing up and down her arms and along her biceps, generating even more warmth in her body. It wasn't just the touch. It was *his* touch.

"I understand that you don't want to come with me for the whole winter. You have a life you need to start here. That makes sense. But could I call you when I'm done with my travels? Maybe swing by to see you?" His expression turned serious in the dim light coming off the porch. "I like you, Selina. I like you a lot."

Her chest swelled at that news, puffing out with pleasure until she was afraid she would pop the zipper on her coat. Thinking he liked her had been one thing; hearing him say it filled a different need entirely.

"I didn't just want you along with me for company and the chance that we would have sex again, just so you know . . ." he continued. "I wanted you along because I think we could have been something. That maybe there was a future here."

His phrasing saddened her, his use of the past tense.

"I like you, too, Marc. But you don't have a future. You're not even sure you want one. You want your past, and I don't exist in your past."

Her words must have stunned him, because he blinked several times, his mouth open and his teeth glinting in the sun. "God, Selina," he said finally. "When you put it like that . . ."

She put her right hand over his as it rested on her left arm, enjoying the length of his bare fingers and the way he gripped her bicep. She wanted so much for him to say that he would stay, set up some sort of Internet company in Salt Lake City, and take her out to dinner, on a real date. But it had to be what he wanted, not what he felt like he had to do.

"I want to settle down," she said. "All I've ever wanted is a good job that I could be proud of, one that paid me enough to buy a house, and have a family. Travel, but for vacation, not because I need to wander. I'm a person who stays put, grows roots. Only Athol wasn't a place I wanted to stay."

She stepped closer, until they were touching, and he wrapped his arms around her. She pressed her head against his chest. "I'm not going to wait for you, but if you ever decided that's what you want, too, give me a call. It doesn't even have to be in Salt Lake City. Just give me a call."

He kissed her hair, then she straightened up to face to him and he brushed his lips against her. She could almost stay like this, safe in his arms forever, the breath from his nose hot on her cool face.

But this was a good-bye kiss. There would be no

nibbling on her bottom lip or exploring his mouth with her tongue. Whatever happened here—kiss included—wouldn't end in anything other than them parting ways.

So she pulled away before she gave in to the temptation to get her bags from inside and follow him to the ends of the Earth.

"That's good-bye, then," he said, looking down at her, dampness in his eyes.

"And thank you." She stepped out of his grip, wrapping her own arms around her for comfort and warmth. He reached out for her again, but she stepped back again. One of them had to do it. She could be the strong one if necessary.

He must have gotten the hint because he nodded. "Thank you for coming with me on this journey. I'm not sure where I'll end up come summer, but I know that the past couple days with you have had a profound effect on me. If I end up doing something else great, it will be because I listened to you. If I don't, it will be because I wasn't smart enough to take your advice."

She smiled even though her heart felt as though it was cracking in millions of pieces. "Good-bye, Marc."

He opened his mouth to say something, then apparently thought better of it, turned and got in his car.

She didn't let herself cry as he drove away.

Chapter Twelve

THERE WAS NO denying that Marc's room at Snowdance was nice. When he'd started this trip, he'd have been thrilled at the space, the expansive views of the mountain, and the luxury of his surroundings. But now he'd rather be back at the middling hotel off a freeway exit in Jerome, Idaho. At least then Selina had been with him.

And Selina had made all the difference in his life.

The bellhop stashed Marc's bags where Marc had asked him to, then left with a generous tip. Marc tossed his backpack onto one of the queen beds, then flopped onto the other. The vast emptiness of the room stretched out from the bed to the mountains, echoing back off the snow. God, he wished Selina were here. But she didn't want to be with him.

No, he corrected himself. He shoved up to a sitting position and forced himself to get up and walk over to the window. Selina wasn't here because what she wanted in her future was different from what he wanted in his future.

Only that wasn't true, either. He didn't know what

he wanted in his future. He could have stayed in Salt Lake with her. It's not like he had to be anywhere at any particular time. But it wasn't fair to her to use her to keep him entertained and distracted while he found himself.

Whatever that meant.

Here you are, he thought as he looked out over the slopes that would be covered in skiers tomorrow. He would be skiing tomorrow, too, and the next day, and the next, and the next . . .

When he thought about it that way, his future stretched out into a long stretch of skiing and driving between resorts. What had sounded like a dream a couple of months ago now sounded like a life sentence.

Selina was right. He wasn't looking for a future in all his travels. He was trying to not commit himself in case his past called him back. He wanted to be able to leap when that phone call came asking for his help.

He pressed his head against the cold windowpane. It wasn't that he didn't believe Curtis and the team he now headed couldn't do the work to keep their baby afloat, or even that Marc was angry over being left out. He had *chosen* not to take a position with the company that had bought their platform. With all that money on the table and the chimera of freedom beckoning, he'd thought moving on to something new was what he wanted.

Moving on was a hell of a lot scarier than staying put.

All the more reason to admire Selina and the guts

she'd shown to get in his car and find a new place to live.

He banged his head against the window until his headache reminded him that his head was better used for thinking than as a hammer.

As he was digging through his backpack for his laptop, the phone in his pocket buzzed with a text message. Curtis. A name he'd not seen in his texting app since Marc had started sending him e-mails about key exchanges.

Interested in work?

Marc's heart began to pound.

Yes!

Not our project. That's done.

God, text messaging could be so annoying for conversations like this. Seeing one small sentence pop across his screen and wondering what would follow but having to wait for it was the worst.

Group working on improved mobile security for banking. Focused on banks in developing countries. Want more info?

Marc tossed the phone to the bed. Mobile banking security was . . .

He was going to say boring, but the more he thought about it, the less boring it seemed. He'd read enough stories in the news about the importance of mobile banking in developing countries to know that something so simple could change the lives of millions. No, billions of people.

He grabbed the phone.

E-mail me.

Not that his decision was made, but he could at least start doing research.

MARC SKIED WHILE he was at Snowdance. He'd paid for the skis, the room, and the lift tickets. Plus, it was fun. But he skipped the pool in favor of room service and lots of time spent in front of his laptop, doing research and negotiating positions. He found the hotel's business room where he could print for exorbitant amounts of money and use a scanner. He contacted old computer geek friends for information and got put in touch with some new contacts with experience in mobile banking.

By the time the end of the week rolled around, Marc was barely able to bend his knees after all the skiing, but he had a new job lined up and ideas on how to improve security in mobile banking while keeping the application flexible enough to be used across countries with various cultural expectations of banking and money.

Ideas that would translate into months and months of work to get off the ground and perfect, followed by years of tweaking as technology changed.

Marc shoved his dirty ski clothes into his bag, not

able to remember when he'd last been so excited to sit in front of a computer for hours on end. The best part of the job was that it would give him stability and something to work on, but the international goal of the work meant he'd also have an excuse to travel.

As he zipped up the bag, he wondered if Selina would see the compromise. He needed one more week to wrap everything up and pin down his future, and then he'd call her.

No. Better yet, he would stop by her house and talk to her.

He wasn't doing this for her, but that didn't mean he wasn't hoping she would be one of the benefits.

SELINA STAGGERED INTO Pam's house, her feet aching from being on them all day. She'd worked a double shift today at the restaurant downtown, which was hard but necessary. In the past couple of weeks since Marc had left, she'd registered for spring classes at the local community college, talked with the gallery owner about a possible job there, and landed herself a waitressing job. All the while, she helped Pam around the house.

She sighed as she pulled her shoes off her feet and wiggled her toes. Not only did the work add money to her bank account but it kept her mind off her loneliness. Pam was good company, too. Selina had gone out to coffee once with one of her coworkers also. But none of them distracted her from the fact that she missed Marc.

With a sigh, she stood up and shuffled to the bathroom to brush her teeth. It would all get easier, she told herself. One day.

Chapter Thirteen

SELINA WAS ABOUT to hang an ornament on Pam's tree when the doorbell rang. She nestled the fragile ornament—a white china bird's nest—back into its small piece of protective wrap and went to the front door to answer it.

Her jaw dropped when she opened it. Marc stood on the other side, a knit cap pulled tight over his floppy hair and his hands shoved into the pockets of a navy peacoat. He no longer looked like a white knight.

Over the course of two weeks, she'd come to realize that falling in love with a white knight was a bad idea. Better to come to a man as an equal than for him to know that he'd rescued you because you weren't able to rescue yourself.

"I don't remember you having a peacoat," she said.

His face broke out into a lopsided grin. "You didn't see all my clothing."

"No, but . . ." *I didn't think you were the peacoat type.*

Really, though, what did she know about him? She'd wondered that every night when crying to herself about her loss. What *had* she lost?

She'd lost a funny, interesting, smart, and capable guy who'd kept all of his promises, never asking for more than she could give, nor offering more than he could follow through on. Along with learning about the dangers of white knights, Pam had also been lecturing about why that trait was so rare, in men and in women.

His brow raised until it nearly touched the ribbing at the bottom of his cap. "No, but?"

"I'm happy to see you," she said because it was true. "But I don't know why you're here." That was true, too.

"Can I come in? I brought you a present."

Selina stepped aside, and Marc passed through the doorway into the entryway of Pam's house. She saw him reappraising the small cottage, now made brighter with an overflow of Christmas decorations, including a large collection of nutcrackers.

"Did I hear the door?" Pam asked, coming through to the living room from the kitchen, a tray of snacks and two mugs of hot chocolate on it.

"Oh," she said, the chocolate sloshing over the sides of the mugs as she stopped short. "It's the young man who brought you here. I was given the impression that you'd left forever."

"I'd hoped you would come back," Selina explained, "but I told you I wasn't going to wait on you." Even though the temptation had been great. Instead, she'd focused her crying on healing and let Pam's excitement over having Selina help putting up the Christmas decorations take her mind off the fact that she no longer had Marc to talk to.

But the man she faced when she turned back from watching Pam leave the room was different. The vulnerability etched in his face didn't make him look older, but it made him look more serious. That was a man she could believe would both put together a multimillion-dollar computer program and go on to do other things with his life, a man looking to plan his future rather than a permanent vacation.

"Selina," he said, his hands outstretched toward her, "you were right. Traveling wasn't what I wanted. Or, maybe I want to travel, but I don't want traveling to be my life. I want to *do* something."

He took a step closer to her. "You were right. About all of it. And I didn't realize it until I was at Snowdance, in this beautiful room with the most amazing view of the mountains I've ever seen and I felt as lost and empty as I ever have. I want to work. I *like* to work. I find meaning in work, where I can build something."

Her heart stilled with his words, hoping that they meant something more than what he was literally saying. Then she took a deep breath and remembered the man she'd spent a couple of days with. He'd been more than his words, and he'd stuck to all his words.

"What does this mean?" she asked.

"It means I want to take you out to dinner. On a date."

She couldn't help but smile. "I think I got that part."

"Is that a yes?"

"I meant, what does this mean for you? Are you looking for work?"

"Huh? Oh. Um, no." He shook his head. "Work found me. Curtis called."

"So you're working on your project again?"

"No. That's the best part." His previously concerned face was now as animated as she had ever seen it. He was clearly more excited about his current project than he ever had been about spending a winter traveling from resort to resort.

"There's a group that's trying to develop better mobile security for banking, specifically for third-world countries where mobile banking is a community's lifeline and can mean the difference between poverty and security for a woman selling baskets or cloth."

"But . . ." Her nervousness returned. "That sounds like something you need to do . . . somewhere else." Salt Lake had an international airport, but you still have to fly somewhere else first to fly internationally.

He waved her concern away. "This is the computer industry. And it's software, not hardware. I can work with anyone, anywhere as long as we both have Internet access. I'll have to travel, yes. You should know that going in. Maybe a lot, even. But I've got an apartment here and I plan to return here. Always."

Her head lifted and dropped and lifted and dropped, slowly as if what he was saying was a ball and she had to roll it into the hole where it would hit a lightbulb and she would understand the importance of what he was saying.

"We could get you a passport," he said, stepping forward, his hands still extended. She slipped her palms into his. "You said you wanted to travel for vacation. Maybe I'll be someplace you want to vacation and you could come with me for a week or two."

Flop. Bang. Ring.

The ball rolling around in her head dropped, and suddenly she got it.

Tears sprang to her eyes as she shuffled closer to him, desperate to touch him and yet afraid that if she let go of his hands, he would disappear and this would all be a dream.

He cocked his head, examining her face. "Are you crying?"

"Yes, but it's because I'm happy." She sniffled. "If you haven't noticed, I'm a crier."

"Oh, I noticed." His wide smile was the embodiment of joy. "Is this a yes?"

"Yes," she said, nodding and sniffling again and then tilting her head up for a kiss. She didn't know if she was agreeing to a date, or a kiss, or the future he'd outlined, but she didn't care. She wanted them all.

Almost instantly, she was wrapped in his arms, their lips pressed together. Their kiss was hopeful, as if they had decades of kisses to set the tone for. When they finally pulled away from each other, Marc looked down at her, his eyes soft with the same love she felt warming her heart.

"Merry Christmas," he said, reaching in to the pocket of his peacoat and pulling out an envelope. "Your present . . ."

Her eyes widened. "What is it?"

He just shrugged so she flipped the envelope over. She tried to be gentle, but the paper ripped as she pushed her finger under the flap. Inside the envelope were two brochures and two cards, which she fanned out in front of her.

"Are these . . . ?"

"Lifetime memberships to the Salt Lake art museums. I didn't know which one to get, so I got both of the big ones. You can volunteer or get a job in a gallery, but this way you can visit anytime you want, too. They were going to be yours even if you sent me packing."

She hugged the envelope to her chest. Even if she decided working in the art world wasn't for her, he was giving her the gift of art. And while he may have given her dreams to her in an envelope, he was a solid, flesh and blood man who wanted to be with her.

And she wanted to be with him. No matter what.

"Merry Christmas," she echoed, reaching up to her tiptoes to drop a kiss on his cheek.

WANT TO READ MORE?

A week skiing in the mountains of Utah is the perfect way for Cassie Sumner to mark the start of her post-divorce life. Especially when the mountains aren't the only gorgeous view . . . But hitting the jackpot with her hot ski instructor doesn't mean she's ready for—or interested in—the vacation fling her best friend is encouraging her to have.

One bad experience years ago was enough for Doug Vanderholt to swear off affairs with students. And he's keeping that promise, even if he can't stop thinking about Cassie's smile. He's remade his life and is only interested in something serious and real.

Doug and Cassie can't ignore their attraction to each other, and they both feel they can just get it out of their systems. But as the week draws to a close and their physical attraction turns deeper, they start to wonder if they can turn a vacation fling into something more.

Buy a copy of *Four Nights to Forever* today!

THANK YOU, READERS!

I appreciate the time you took to read *Twelve Kisses Until Christmas*. Authors love reviews and I'm not different. Whether you liked the book or hated it, all online reviews are great.

You can find me online at my website, on Facebook, and on Twitter. Sign up for my newsletter for occasional updates and information about upcoming books.

Website: jenniferlohmann.com
Facebook: facebook.com/iferlohmann
Twitter: twitter.com/iferlohmann
Newsletter: jenniferlohmann.com/contact-jennifer-lohmann

THANK YOU, MOLLY!

This anthology this novella was written for was Molly's idea, way back at RWA in San Antonia in 2014. I've loved working with this group of women and hope to be able to again (hint, hint).

ABOUT THE AUTHOR

Jennifer Lohmann is a Rocky Mountain girl at heart, having grown up in southern Idaho and Salt Lake City. When she's not writing or working as a librarian, she wrangles three evil cats. Fortunately, the boa constrictor is better behaved. She lives in North Carolina with her own personal Viking.